MR. NOT RIGHT FOR HER

COWBOY CONFESSIONS, BOOK #1

JO GRAFFORD

Mr. Not Right for Her

Cover design: Jo Grafford of JG PRESS

ISBN: 978-1-63907-032-9

GET A FREE BOOK!

Join my mailing list to be the first to know about new releases, free books, special discount prices, Bonus Content, and giveaways.

https://BookHip.com/JNNHTK

ACKNOWLEDGMENTS

Many, many thanks to my editor, Cathleen Weaver, for helping me polish this story and make it the best it could be. I also appreciate my super awesome beta readers — Debbie Turner, Mahasani, and Pigchevy. I want to give another shout out to my Cuppa Jo Readers on Facebook. Thank you for reading and loving my books!

CHAPTER 1: ALL TRIPPED UP

ASHER

ASHER CASSIDY AVOIDED LOOKING into mirrors. It wasn't because he couldn't bear the sight of what had happened to him one year ago today, because he could. His parents hadn't raised a sissy. What he couldn't bear each time he saw his own reflection was the reminder that his girlfriend hadn't been able to accept this version of him — a cowboy with scars running from his left temple to his collarbone. As it turned out, a freak fire in an old barn could do a lot of damage to a guy's face.

Jade only paid him a handful of visits at the hospital he'd been air-lifted to in Amarillo, and she'd broken up with him the day he'd finally been discharged. By a lame text message, no less! She didn't even have the decency to do it in person.

Asher jammed his hands in the pockets of his jeans as he stared out the window of his main-level office. It was pouring outside this morning, which was fine with him. The gloomy skies matched his mood. Not to mention, Cassidy Farm could use the rain. The whole town could — all three square miles of the newly incorporated Chipper, Texas.

Feeling nothing like the ridiculously upbeat name of the town he now lived in, he trudged back to his desk to flip on a lamp and take a seat. The fact that his mother had recently replaced his wooden work-bench desk with a chrome executive-style one only added to his irritation. And don't even get him started on his new swivel chair that was upholstered in flame-retardant fabric. His parents had literally gone off the deep end when it came to fire-proofing his environment. Ever since the fire, they'd been investing in a frenzy of upgrades — new electrical wiring, state-of-the-art appliances, and what not. The building he now worked in looked like it was constructed of traditional red barn slats, but every inch of it was steel.

Then they'd taken it one huge step further. They'd circulated a petition to transform their small farming community into its own township, where they were currently in the process of recruiting and training their own fire department. Yeah, he understood their reasons. He scrubbed a hand over his scarred cheek. And, no, he didn't blame them. However, the address change alone had created dozens of hours of paper-work. As the oldest of their six sons and the manager of Cassidy Farm, he was the lucky guy responsible for updating the address of their family-owned busi-ness on, well, everything — from tax forms, to vendor accounts, to you name it.

And despite his mother's constant nagging, he didn't have so much as a part-time administrative assistant to help him tackle the ever-growing pile of address-change forms. His fault, of course, since he'd refused to hire any of her friends' daughters and granddaughters she'd nudged in his direction. No way was he putting up with any more than he absolutely had to of all the nose-wrinkling pity and inadvertent little cringes females tended to give every time they looked at his face.

"Um, hello?" The soft questioning voice made Asher's head jerk toward the doorway.

A slender figure stood there with the ends of her dark braids dripping. She wore a straw Stetson glistening with raindrops and a soggy red and black plaid shirt that was hanging open and clinging to her black t-shirt underneath. Her faded jeans were spattered with yet more dampness, and her leather boots made a squishing sound as she shifted her weight from one foot to the other.

Wondering what a scraggly teenager was doing at his office door, Asher waved a hand impatiently in the direction of his family's store and coffee shop. He purposefully kept his face averted, more out of habit than anything else, so she couldn't see the scars. "Our store is inside the next building over." His tone was dismissive. He'd never seen her before. Probably some tourist passing through, one who'd bumbled into his office by mistake.

"Oh, I wasn't going shopping, sir. I'm, ah…here for my interview." She pushed the door open a little wider, taking a half step into the room. The movement was accompanied by another squishing sound.

"Interview!" He wrinkled his brow at her. *What interview?* He'd just this morning posted the job opening for a new ranch hand on their company website, but that was only an hour ago. He definitely hadn't set up any interviews yet.

"Yes, sir. For the ranch hand position. The lady at the cash register pointed me this way."

But, of course, she did. He gave a grim nod of understanding. *Thank you, Mom.* He loved the woman dearly, but Claire Cassidy's impulsive nature had a way of wearing him down to the bone sometimes. It probably hadn't occurred to her to pick up the phone and call her oldest son before sending a perfect stranger marching into his office. She was forever bemoaning how she missed the days when he'd worked inside the store in a room she'd since converted to a storage closet. Back then, all anyone had to do was poke their head around the door and give a holler if they wanted something from him. Nowadays, he was a short hike away in an adjacent building. Initially, Asher had enjoyed the extra privacy, but his mother was forever finding new and creative ways to work around it.

Hence, the job candidate currently dripping puddles in the doorway of his office.

"Come on in, Miss ah...I didn't catch your name." He stood to usher his unexpected guest into the room, fully intending to reschedule their meeting to a more convenient time. He couldn't have been less in the mood to conduct a job interview.

"Bella Johnson," she supplied, pushing back her Stetson as she stepped forward. The gesture had the unfortunate result of draining the rest of the water from the brim of her hat onto the floor behind her. "Omigosh!" Her freckled cheeks flushed with embarrassment. "I'm so sorry. It's pretty wet outside. Here, I'll clean it up." Glancing nervously around the room, her gaze zeroed in on the roll of paper towels mounted below a set of storage cabinets just inside the door. His mother had put her head next to the architects's and designed the space herself. The floor-to-ceiling nook had all the features of a full-fledged kitchenette, complete with a microwave and mini stovetop combo, a lower cabinet fridge, a separate glassed-in beverage fridge, a sink with filtered water, an ice maker, and an espresso machine with so many options it could probably be programmed to clean the entire room.

He watched his would-be job candidate squish-walk her way over to the paper towel dispenser, tear a handful of sheets from the roll, and squish-walk her way back to the doorway.

Behind her back, he gestured indignantly at the damp footprints she left on his hardwood floor. It was as if her boots were bleeding water.

However, she didn't seem to notice the additional mess she'd made as she stooped over to clean up the rather impressive puddle her hat had made.

A commotion outside the door made her pause her dabbing and glance up in alarm.

A man's voice shouted something. It was followed by the frenzied barking of a dog.

Uh-oh. Asher recognized the sounds all too well. It was his youngest brother, Fox, and his latest rescue pet, a German Shepherd named Ghost. The all-white dog had wandered onto their two-hundred acre farm about a month ago, his fur matted with stickers and blood. Fox had nursed him back to health, and the two of them had become fast friends. He was having a little less luck in the area of instilling the creature with any meaningful training or discipline. And the fact that he was yapping and scrambling across the wooden flooring outside Asher's office meant he was taking advantage of someone leaving the barn door open.

The most likely culprit of said crime was currently squatting over the puddle on his floor. However, he'd address that issue in a bit. First, he had an unsuspecting stranger to get out of the line of fire.

"Shut the door!" he hollered to her. Forgetting about the need to keep his face averted from the would-be ranch hand, he lurched in her direction.

She spun toward him, half-rising from her crouch. Her eyes rounded like twin blue-gray lakes as they fastened on his scars. Her split-second hesitation in following his order was all it took for Ghost's flying front paws to breach the open doorway. The enormous dog sailed joyfully through the air in the direction of the nearest human, who just so happened to be the bedraggled Miss Bella Johnson.

Asher, who was already dashing out from behind his desk, barely made it across the room in time to cushion the young woman against the dog's impact. The German Shepherd slammed his front paws between her shoulder blades, dropping a sloppy kiss on her right earlobe and knocking her hat to the floor. She squealed in surprise and fell forward, hands flailing, into Asher's outstretched arms.

Most unfortunately, he'd chosen today of all days to break in a new pair of snake skin boots. As he took a step back for leverage, the yet un-scuffed sole of his right boot landed in a patch of water and skidded a few inches.

The three of them went hurtling toward the floor — man, woman, and dog. Asher landed on the bottom of the pile, and the massive white dog landed on top, forming a gasping female sandwich out of the hapless job candidate his mother had sent his way.

Asher's heart pounded harder while visions of liability lawsuits danced through his mind. However, it wasn't his most immediate concern. The woman in his arms seemed to be having trouble breathing. He couldn't tell if she'd had the wind knocked out of her or worse.

"Miss Johnson," he cried, irritably nudging the dog's head away from hers. "Are you alright?" He finally managed to sit up. It wasn't an easy task with Ghost climbing all over them, dripping rainwater and barking to wake the dead.

To Asher's alarm, Bella Johnson pressed her forehead to his shoulder, her whole body trembling.

Good gravy! She was going into shock. Fearing she'd hit her head on the way down, Asher no longer cared what it was going to cost his company. She needed medical care, and she needed it now.

Fox barreled into the room with a harried look plastered to his angular features. A lock of brown hair fell over his eyes as he dove for his dog. "Sorry, y'all. I was leash training him on the front porch of the store, and he got away from me. Ghost, my man," he scolded, reaching the dog and hauling him off of Bella Johnson. "Some days you're more trouble than you're worth."

"Some days?" Asher shot his youngest sibling an incredulous look. "More like every day!" He returned his attention to their guest, gently probing her scalp for injuries. "Can you tell me where it hurts, ma'am?"

Her shoulders shook harder. "In my dignity, if that counts." She slowly raised her flaming face from his shoulder.

That was when he realized that the sounds she'd been making weren't from struggling to breathe. She was convulsed in silent laughter.

As she watched his agonized concern morph into profound relief, she laughed harder.

He shook his head, not quite sure what to make of her behavior. Up this close, a few things were more readily apparent than when she'd been standing in his doorway. Bella Johnson wore no make-up to accentuate her wide eyes, dark lashes, and high cheekbones. Furthermore, she wasn't as young as he'd originally supposed, probably not as old as his own twenty-nine years but definitely not a teenager. Lastly, she wasn't merely shaking with laughter. Her clothing was soaked through and through, and her fingers gripping his shoulders felt icy through the fabric of his shirt.

Spring had sprung a few days ago in the Texas panhandle, but this morning's rain had cooled down the outdoors all over again. Asher wondered why the woman sprawled across his lap wasn't wearing a raincoat. She didn't seem to be in possession of an umbrella, either. But before he could inquire into her circumstances, the two of them were pelted with yet more water droplets. This time, it was Ghost's fault.

The dog was hunkered down a few feet away, fiercely shaking the rain from his furry white coat. It sprayed everywhere. Asher wouldn't have been surprised if a few drops landed in the coffee mug on his desk.

Without thinking, he banded his arms around the shivering woman in his lap, trying to shield her from the worst of it. "So help me, Fox!" he growled. "If you don't get that mutt out of here..."

"We're gone," his youngest brother assured hastily, dragging the protesting dog from the office.

Asher didn't relax his grip on the woman in his embrace until he heard the creature barking his way down the hallway.

"Worst interview ever," Bella Johnson moaned in a laughing voice against his neck.

It took him an extra moment to realize he had her head tucked beneath his chin on the side where his worst burn scars rested. He stiffened and drew back a few inches to scowl down at her.

"I'm sorry," she said softly.

"What for?" For the life of him, he couldn't see how Ghost's untimely appearance was in any way her fault. Fox had just finished explaining how the dog had escaped his leash training. Asher's biggest concern right now was that she'd sustained injuries she wasn't yet owning up to.

"For leaving the door open, and for bringing a stream of water as wide as the Mississippi River into your office." Another giggle escaped her. "Oh, and for laughing when I shouldn't have. I do that some-times," she confessed ruefully. "It's easier than having a melt-down when life serves you a few lemons." Her choice of words made Asher more curious than ever about her story. Though she didn't elaborate, she finally grew sober. Or tried to. A wobbly smile continued to curve her lips as she met his gaze.

Her mouth was as damp as the rest of her, but with lip gloss instead of water. Cherry, from the scent of it. The brief glance Asher allowed himself to give them revealed they were lush and kissable lips. He wasn't sure where that thought had come from, though it was a stark reminder of how long it had been since his last date — a little over a year.

"Are you hurt, sir?" she blurted suddenly. A stricken look clouded her gaze as she scrambled to climb out of his lap. "I was so busy laughing and dodging raindrops that I—"

"I'm fine," he interrupted, curling forward to his feet. His backside was a little bruised, but no way was he admitting that.

To his surprise, she held out a hand to assist him. Though it was entirely unnecessary, he reached for it to be polite and was struck all over again by the coolness of her fingers.

Using his own strength to curl forward to his feet, the cramp in his leg caught him by surprise, making him stumble on his way to the coffee dispenser.

He could feel Bella Johnson's gaze on him. "Did you serve in the military, sir?"

"Nope." He had no interest in talking about his injuries. During the fire, he'd been pinned beneath a fallen beam when the loft over the horse stalls had collapsed. The residual cramping was from the previously shattered bones in his calf, a torn Achilles, and nerve damage. It had taken surgery and many months of convalescing for the bones and surrounding muscle tissue to heal. The nerves were still in the process of regenerating. However, he wasn't complaining. He considered himself fortunate to still have the leg. Most importantly, he'd managed to rescue the horses that had been trapped inside the burning building before becoming immobilized himself.

"So, ah...about my interview, sir..." Bella's voice

brought him back to the damp and chilly present.

"You can drop the sir," he informed her in a clipped tone. It seemed to him that the time for formalities between them was past. He was as wet as Fox's mutt, and probably smelled like him, too. "I'm Asher Cassidy, ranch manager." He reached for a pair of mugs and brewed two fresh cups beneath his double dispenser. The mugs were white porcelain with the Cassidy Farm logo affixed in raised relief — a tarnished metal horse's head with a flowing mane surrounded by a wreath of silver corn stalks.

"Nice to meet you, sir. I mean, Mr. Cassidy," she corrected hastily.

"Asher," he supplied blandly. "We go by first names around here." Grimacing, he leaned on the coffee bar with both hands to stretch out the tendons in his bum leg. It mostly acted up on cold mornings like this morning. The rest of the time, it was okay.

"Are you sure I didn't hurt you?" Bella Johnson inquired in an anxious voice. "I'm a lot heavier than I look, which is probably why I knocked you clean over."

He couldn't resist glancing over his shoulder to curl his lip at her. What a preposterous claim! She couldn't be more than a hundred pounds sopping wet. "I slid on the water."

"Oh, gosh! I'm so sorry about that, too." A hand flew to her mouth. "So, so, so sorry!"

"Sit, Miss Johnson." Ignoring her dramatic outburst, he angled his head at the pair of armchairs in front of his desk.

"I can't. I'm too wet." She stooped to retrieve her hat. "But thanks, anyway." She clapped her soggy hat back on her head. "I thought you said you go by first names around here, so I'm Bella. Just Bella. And don't worry. I'm not expecting an interview at this point."

Too bad, because that's exactly what you're going to get. Like it or not, her pre-screening was well underway. "The chairs are covered in synthetic leather." He handed her one of the steaming mugs in his hands. "Whether you stay for the interview is entirely your choice. Regardless, I need you to take a seat so we can file an incident report. Any medical expenses you incur as a result of the injuries you sustained in my office today will be covered by Cassidy Farm."

Looking amused, she accepted the mug of coffee. "I'm not hurt, thanks to you. Not sure you can say the same thing." Still shivering, she studied him critically as she finally took a seat in front of his desk.

Not seeing what business his condition was to her, he limped over to one of his storage closets to retrieve his navy rain jacket. On his way back to his desk, he paused by the thermostat to tap it up a few degrees. Then he returned to Bella's side to drape his jacket around her shoulders.

"Thanks," she murmured, reaching up to tug the ends of it more snugly around her chin.

"I assume you brought a resume with you?" He was no longer interested in rescheduling her interview. For one thing, he wasn't sure his office would survive another one of her cyclone entrances. Best to get it over with now and end their disastrous encounter once and for all.

"Um, yes. Just a sec." Setting her mug on the edge of his desk, she stood and hurried from the room.

He took a seat behind his desk, staring curiously after her.

She returned moments later with a backpack — a huge, sporty looking red one — and a guitar, of all things. It was encased in a hard black plastic shell, a good thing considering the weather. "Here." She unzipped her backpack and withdrew a manilla folder. Removing a single sheet of paper from it, she slid it across the desk in his direction.

He scanned the contents of her resume while sipping his coffee. What he read made him take a bigger gulp than he intended, scalding his tongue. "You're a school teacher?" He abruptly set down his mug. Why in tarnation was a high school music teacher from Dallas applying to become a lowly ranch hand? It made zero sense. That is, unless she'd done something to get herself fired. His suspicions stirred.

"Was," she corrected coolly, "before I came to my senses and turned in my resignation."

"Come again?" He frowned at her. It wasn't the answer he'd been expecting, but it was better than finding out she'd been let go for the heinous treatment of minors or some other offense that would render her unhireable.

She made a face. "When was the last time you set foot inside a public school?"

He did a quick mental calculation. "Does college count?" It had been twelve years since he'd graduated from high school, but he'd attended a few in-person classes as part of his accounting degree from a state college. The rest of his coursework he'd finished online.

"Not even," she scoffed. "By that point, they've weeded out most of the future felons."

"I see." It was an interesting description for teenagers, one he'd never heard before. He couldn't tell if she was joking, so he waited for whatever outrageous thing she would say next.

"I don't think you do." She sniffed in disdain. "Clearly, it's been a while since you last visited a high school. Not sure why they even call us teachers, because you do precious little teaching in the classroom these days. It's mostly crowd control." She gave a gusty sigh that he gauged as one part wistfulness and two parts regret.

"That bad, huh?" It was the most unusual interview he'd ever conducted. Oddly enough, it was also the most enjoyable. For one thing, the job candidate sitting in front of him wasn't paying the least bit of attention to his scars. For this reason, he'd all but forgotten to keep them averted from her.

"Worse," she declared darkly, though she chose not to expound on that titillating point.

It made him wonder what kind of district she'd taught in. It certainly didn't sound like the small country high school less than a mile down the road, from which all six Cassidy brothers had graduated.

He honestly couldn't remember anything worse happening there than an occasional food fight in the cafeteria. That was back when it had been called County Line High School, of course. It had since been renamed Chipper High, home of the Coyotes, wild and ravenous creatures that were all too plentiful in the surrounding canyons. His brother Beldon was constantly on the lookout for them during his range riding patrols.

At Bella's lapse into silence, Asher cleared his throat. "So, tell me." It was time to return their conversation to the job in question. "How does anything on your resume translate into being a ranch hand?" For the life of him, he couldn't make the connection. After teaching high school, it appeared she'd meandered her way through the state, playing music at churches and sporting events while serving as a seasonal farm worker. Okay, that last part was a little more relevant to the job skills he was looking for. It still didn't prove she had what it took to work with animals, though. *Shoot!* He'd just finished watching an eighty-five pound dog send her sprawling.

"That's simple." She gave a wry chuckle. "It's my opinion that anyone who can survive three straight years in a public school classroom can do anything they set their mind to."

He did a quick mental calculation and estimated that three years of teaching following a four-year college degree put Bella somewhere in the vicinity of twenty-five-years-old. Narrowing his gaze on hers, he pressed, "You do realize that a ranch hand's responsibilities include mucking stalls, right?"

She didn't bat an eyelash. "I can handle whatever you throw at me, Asher Cassidy. Hire me, and I'll prove it." Another shiver belied her tough-sounding words, though. She reached for her coffee mug again, cupping it with both hands as she lifted it to her mouth. She seemed as eager to absorb the heat of the steaming beverage as she was to drink it.

"Anything, huh?" Pursing his lips in consideration, he lounged back in his swivel chair, crossing his arms.

"Anything," she repeated with conviction. She bent her face over the coffee and breathed deeply, as if savoring the scent.

He'd have to check her references first, but he was starting to think he might have found the perfect answer to his most immediate hiring need — the personal assistant he'd yet to start advertising for. Sure, there were more qualified candidates out there for the stuff that needed to be done around the farm, but there probably wasn't a single ranch hand on the planet who could more easily jump into the other pressing projects he had in mind, beginning with all those blasted address-change forms piling up on his desk.

"How long are you planning on sticking around?" He unfolded his arms and abruptly sat forward to pin Bella with a hard look. This was the part where they got down to business and talked turkey.

She shrugged. "I could lie and give you the text-book answer you're looking for, but I've always preferred to tell the truth." She sat forward, mimicking his rigidly determined posture. "The truth is easier to live with, even if it gets me booted straight out of this interview."

Asher moved his finger in a circle to urge her on, impatient for her to continue. Her resume all but stated she was a rolling stone. However, that wasn't necessarily a bad thing in his book. His mother had been riding his case for months about hiring an office assistant, and this was one way to check off that box without any permanent strings attached. If things didn't work out with Bella Johnson, she'd already have one foot out the door.

She raised and lowered her shoulders. "I'm one of those people who thinks everything happens for a reason. So, here I am," she finished simply.

Well, that was a non-answer if he'd ever heard one. He had no more idea why Bella Johnson wanted to come work for him than he had when she'd first walked through his door. Clearly, she had stuff in her past she didn't want to talk about. That much was obvious. But so did he. He hoped it meant they could work together with a minimal amount of chit-chat.

"Assuming your references check out, how soon will you be able to start?" He drummed his fingers on his desk as he mentally ran through the inprocessing forms and tasks he'd need to complete with her. *Yay. More paperwork.*

Her expression didn't change. "Immediately."

Again, it wasn't the answer he'd been expecting. "You sure you don't need a few days to relocate and such?" He imagined she had an apartment somewhere between Dallas and here that was full to overflowing with feminine belongings.

She pointed at the two items resting beside her chair. "Everything I own is in my backpack and guitar case."

"You're kidding!" He scowled as another thought struck him. "Are you in any trouble?"

"Define trouble." The stare she fixed on him was pure innocence.

He couldn't believe she was making him spell it out for her. "Are you running from something?" he supplied dryly. "Or someone?" Like an abusive ex. The thought came out of nowhere, making his jaw tighten.

Unless he was mistaken, she paled a little. However, her grin from earlier returned in full force. "Not that I'm aware of." She lifted her chin. "Feel free to dig as long as you want into my background, but the worst you'll find is that I'm flat broke and in desperate need of a job. Last time I checked, neither of those things were crimes."

He nodded thoughtfully, feeling like they were finally getting somewhere. Being broke would certainly explain Bella Johnson's meager belongings. It also meant she wasn't likely to turn down any reasonable job offer. He felt an unholy sense of glee at the realization that she'd inadvertently handed him the upper hand in the interview.

"Like I mentioned earlier," he drawled, watching her expression closely, "the job I'm about to offer you is entirely contingent upon your references checking out."

Her expression brightened at his mention of a forthcoming offer of employment. "They will. I guarantee it." Her words were followed by another shiver.

Knowing he needed to conclude the interview so she could change into dry clothing, he stated an hourly pay rate that made her eyes turn luminous and her lips part in surprise.

"That's nearly twice the amount you listed on your job posting," she gasped.

Though her response was the one he'd hoped for, he kept his expression carefully deadpan. "I believe it was labeled as our starting rate, and your particular skill set justifies coming in a bit higher. Your benefits package will include one of the loft rooms in the horse barn, though you're more than welcome to find a place of your own in town." The original floor plan had called for a pair of upper-level dorm rooms for hired hands. However, his mother had insisted on dividing the space into a series of individual studio apartments instead. He was more appreciative than ever of her forward thinking, considering the fact he was about to hire their first female employee ever.

"What's the catch?" Bella's smile was still pasted on, but it no longer reached her eyes. "Pardon my pessimism, but your offer sounds a little too good to be true."

Glad you asked. He pointed to the pile of address change forms on his desk. "You said you could handle anything I throw your way. That's the catch. I'm hiring you to handle anything I wake up and decide to assign you each day. That means you'll be mucking stalls, milking cows, driving a baler during hay season, and occasionally helping out here in the office." Which, incidentally, would entail working alongside a boss with a severely ravaged face.

"So, I'll only be a ranch hand some of the time," she mused. "The rest of the time I'll be serving as what? Your personal assistant?"

"Yep." He averted his face again to hide his scars. "With a resume like yours, I'm willing to pay you more than I would for a ranch hand, but only if you're prepared to suffer through a few hours of office work now and then." Knowing he'd driven a bargain she couldn't afford to refuse, he resisted the urge to break into a triumphant whistle. He was about to have an employee at his beck and call every time he snapped his fingers. Literally.

"I accept," she said quietly, still looking a little dazed by his generosity.

"Then welcome aboard." Asher didn't dare smile, though the temptation was strong. The two of them weren't friends and never would be, but that didn't mean he wasn't going to enjoy having someone to pick up the slack around Cassidy Farm.

He could only hope Bella Johnson was as prepared as she claimed to get to work. He certainly didn't intend to go easy on her.

CHAPTER 2: BOSS MAN

BELLA

ASHER CASSIDY PICKED up the phone and dialed someone. "Any chance you can break away long enough to give Bella Johnson a tour of our loft accommodations?"

A female squeal and barrage of words on the other end made him grimace and shift restlessly in his chair. "Yes, I made a tentative job offer." His piercing blue gaze returned to Bella. "Pending her references checking out."

There was another lengthy female response, to which her new boss listened for several moments with barely concealed impatience. "Thanks," he said when he could finally get a word in. "Love you, too." There was no irritation in his final statement as he disconnected the line.

For no easily definable reason, Bella's heart sank a few degrees. Had he just finished speaking with his wife? The fact that he wasn't wearing a wedding ring had led her to assume he wasn't married, but not all guys wore wedding rings. Not that his marital status was any of her business, but…

Less than a minute later, the office door burst open, and the middle-aged woman from behind the cash register glided into the room. "Morning, Asher!" she sang out. Not immediately acknowledging Bella's presence, the petite blonde pranced around the room to throw her arms around him from behind. Planting a loud smooch on top of his head, she finally met Bella's gaze.

"You've decided to try your hand at ranching, eh?"

"Yes, ma'am." Bella's heart lightened at the discovery that the woman Asher adored so much was his own mother.

She stepped away from his chair, beckoning Bella to follow her. "Well, before you change your mind, I'd best show you around." She paused at the front entrance to grab an enormous umbrella from a bucket by the door. "I'll do my best to dash us between the raindrops."

It didn't prove to be too difficult of a task since the rain was letting up. Bella followed the woman down a sidewalk and across a gravel parking lot to reach the next building. Like Asher's office, it boasted freshly painted red slats above a brick knee-wall. Unlike Asher's office, however, it was not another administrative building. It was a horse barn. After depositing her umbrella in a bucket by the door, Claire Cassidy led her between two long rows of horse stalls to a set of stairs in the rear of the barn.

They mounted the stairs together and reached a narrow walkway. On one side was a row of doors. On the other side was a railing overlooking the horse stalls.

"Have you ever lived in a barn?" Mrs. Cassidy tossed a cheery grin over her shoulder.

"I wish." Bella chuckled at her choice of words. "I was actually raised in the city." By her maternal grandparents after losing her single mom in a car pileup during her elementary school years. They'd been her parents in every way that mattered, though. She owed her good old-fashioned upbringing to them. Despite their lack of wealth, they'd taught her the meaning of an honest day's work and had cheered her every step of the way through college. Well, Gram had, anyway. Grandpop had passed in the middle of her junior year. Only Gram had gotten to see Bella walk across the stage to accept her diploma.

Claire Cassidy rapped her knuckles lightly against the doorframe of the first door they came to. As she and Bella stepped across the threshold, she breezed, "It looks like wood, but it's actually steel. The whole building is." She was a petite woman in dark designer blue jeans and a well-tailored red blazer. Her white-on-white striped blouse was meticulously ironed, and every platinum blonde hair was in place.

Standing next to her, Bella felt like a half-drowned rat. It was mortifying the way her boots squished every time she took a step. Maybe it wasn't her brightest idea, after all, to save money on transportation by hiking the last two days. However, there was no way she could've guessed that the twenty-three percent chance for rain that the weather forecasters had predicted would turn into such a deluge.

"It's an absolutely gorgeous apartment." She was more than a little awed as she set her guitar case and backpack on the floor just inside the doorway. Spinning in a slow, squishy circle, she tugged the collar of Asher's jacket more tightly around her shivering frame. "Everything looks so new," she added in awe, having a hard time believing she was going to be staying here rent free.

"Because it is." Claire gave a matter-of-fact nod as she hurried forward to push open the curtains. They were semi-sheer black and white plaid panels that draped all the way to the rustic wood flooring. The surrounding walls were painted a pale gray. Overhead was an iron chandelier fashioned from a riot of deer antlers and candle bulbs.

"Wow!" Bella said, more to herself than to Mrs. Cassidy. She was relieved to note that the studio apartment was already furnished with a queen-sized bed and a pair of nightstands. Otherwise, she would've been on the hardwood floor this evening, using her backpack for a pillow. There was also a bistro table with two high-back stools inside a tiny kitchenette. Against the adjacent wall was a black leather armchair with an end table resting beside it that could easily be transformed into a music practice area. She could already picture her collapsable music stand and guitar looking right at home there.

"Is that a *wow*, as in you like it? Or a *wow*, as in what in the world have you gotten yourself into?" Though Mrs. Cassidy's voice was teasing, there was a concerned wrinkle riding the center of her forehead.

"Oh, I definitely like it." Bella had to pinch her arm to make sure she wasn't dreaming. Like everything else about Cassidy Farm, her living quarters seemed almost too good to be true.

"Good." Mrs. Cassidy sounded both pleased and mildly apologetic. "You're our first female ranch hand, which is why the furnishings are so, well, macho. Feel free to add a little color to the place."

Bella drank in the sight of the clean white comforter and sheets on the bed, seeing no immediate need to redecorate. A patchwork quilt was trifolded and draped across the foot of it, adding a homey touch. "It's perfect," she added softly. It was far nicer than the tiny cottage in the city where she'd spent her high school years, four to five times bigger than her college dorm room had been, and at least twice the size of her first rental home on the humble outskirts of Dallas. And due to wasting her life savings on a custom wedding dress she was never going to wear, she'd only been able to afford the seediest hotel accommodations during her hike across northern Texas.

"Well, I'm glad you think so." Mrs Cassidy shot a curious glance at Bella's backpack and guitar case. "You sure do travel light."

"Always." Bella didn't see any point in informing the woman that she was looking at all of her newest ranch hand's earthly possessions. Asher could tell her if he wanted to. She continued to explore the room, pausing at the two doors to the right of the bed. One turned out to be a spacious walk-in closet. The other was a full bathroom. She gave a delicious shiver at the thought of stepping into a hot shower and finally getting warm again.

"There's a pair of towels and wash cloths in the vanity, plus some sample-sized toiletries in the top drawer on the right." Mrs. Cassidy's voice was kind and welcoming. "Unless you have any other questions, I'll leave you to get settled in." She pointedly eyed the jacket Bella was still clutching around her shoulders.

"Just one question." Bella's face heated at the very real possibility that Asher's mother had recognized the borrowed jacket as belonging to her son. *Awkward!* "Do you have any advice for me as a new employee?"

"Nothing earth-shattering. We mostly value hard work and honesty around here. I'm sure my son made that clear during your interview."

Bella drew a deep breath. No, Asher Cassidy hadn't shed much light on his expectations of her on the job, other than the fact that she'd be handling everything he woke up and decided to assign her. He'd been painfully clear about that detail.

"Thank you, ma'am." She nodded politely, still brimming with unanswered questions. "Oh, and what about a dress code?" Asher hadn't touched on that topic, either. All Bella owned at the moment was another pair of jeans and a few extra shirts, nothing fancy. She intended to do some much-needed clothes shopping with her first paycheck.

Mrs. Cassidy eyed her damp clothing. "What you have on is fine, my dear."

"Even for office work?" Asher had been wearing jeans and boots, too, but his were newer than hers — a lot newer and a lot nicer.

The woman's perfectly manicured eyebrows rose. "After today, you probably won't spend much time inside the office."

Bella nodded, realizing the woman must have no inkling of Asher's intentions to assign her office work in addition to her farm tasks. Then again, they probably didn't have too many school teachers applying for manual labor positions here.

"That said, what you're wearing is still fine," the woman added warmly.

"I'm glad to hear it." Relief flooded Bella. Asher had said she was to report back to him within the hour, at which time they'd be completing the rest of her new hire paperwork. She had no idea yet if she'd be spending the rest of the day in the office or some-place else.

Mrs. Cassidy waved the apartment key in the air. "I'll leave this on the bistro. Any extra copies are five dollars apiece. Lost or stolen ones cost more, since it requires re-keying the door."

"I understand. Thank you again, ma'am."

"You betcha." With one last glance at the navy blue jacket Bella was wearing, Mrs. Cassidy made her exit.

Bella wasted no time hopping in the shower. She turned the water on the hottest setting she could bear without raising a blister and was soon toasty warm again. "Thank you, Lord," she breathed as she lathered shampoo into her hair. After months of wandering, it felt like her difficult existence had finally taken a long-overdue upward turn. Maybe. So long as she could handle working for the unsmiling Asher Cassidy.

She had a sneaking suspicion that staying on his good side was going to require more than the hard work and honesty his mother had mentioned. Whatever calamity had befallen him had left more scars than the ones she could see on his face. He was angry and bitter. A little less obvious was the hurt he tried to hide. The only reason she recognized it was because she was a bit of a subject-matter expert on the topic herself.

On the other hand, he wasn't the first tough boss she'd ever worked for, and he probably wouldn't be the last. She would do what she always did — work her fingers to the bone and earn as much money as she could before her past caught up to her. Then she'd hit the road and do it all over again.

———

Asher held up Bella Johnson's one-page resume and scanned her short list of references. After a moment of deliberation, he decided to call the most relevant one first, the place where she'd served as a seasonal farm worker.

To his surprise, his call was answered right away. "Yeah?" a man barked.

"Hey, this is Ranch Manager Asher Cassidy from Cassidy Farm up in Chipper, Texas." He doubted anyone had ever heard of the newly incorporated township, but he always started off his telephone conversations by disclosing who he was and where he was calling from. "I was hoping to reach Mr. Eli Britt."

"Speaking." The man's voice was impatient.

"I'm calling about a job reference for Miss Bella Johnson."

"Well, if you want my advice, don't hire her." Mr. Britt's voice was spitting anger.

"Whoa!" Asher's heart sank. This was not the conversation he'd been expecting to have after Bella had guaranteed her references would check out. "The fact is, I've already given Miss Johnson a tentative job offer. Would you mind elaborating on why you don't advise me to hire her?"

"Yep. 'Cause she won't last long."

"What do you mean, sir?"

"Can't prove it, but I suspect she's running from something. Pretty sure the reason she left her job so sudden like at my place was because of the feller that came looking for her."

You little fibber! Asher was disappointed to find out that Bella had lied about being in trouble. So far, though, he still hadn't heard a rock solid reason against hiring her altogether. "How was she as an employee?"

"The best there is." There was no hesitation in Mr. Britt's answer. "That's why I'm so out of joint about her leaving. Took two whole other people to replace the work she did."

Nice. Asher doubted that Eli Britt intended for his griping to be taken as a job reference, but that's sure what it sounded like to him. "I'm sorry to hear it, sir."

"You and me both, son. What's worse, she left without collecting her last paycheck or giving me an address where I could send it. Truth be told, the wife and I have been worried sick about what became of her."

"You can send it here," Asher said quickly. "I'll make sure she gets it." *Assuming she stays long enough for the mail to run.*

"That's all fine and dandy, but how do I know you're who you say you are?" The man sounded more exasperated than before. "For all I know, you're the same fellow she's running from."

Good point. "How about I have her call you after lunch on this same number?"

"That oughta do." The farm owner sounded enormously relieved. "I can have her check in the mail today to whatever address she gives me."

"Appreciate that, sir. I'm sure she will, too."

Mr. Britt gave a gusty sigh. "She's a rare find if you can hold on to her. Mr. ah…"

"Cassidy. Asher Cassidy," he repeated.

"I reckon I came on a little strong when I first heard the reason you were calling. To be honest, you could do a lot worse than hiring the likes of her." Mr. Britt sighed again. "I'd hire her back in a heartbeat. The wife and I took a real liking to her."

Asher snorted. Okay, so Bella hadn't lied about her job references checking out, after all. It did sound like she was in trouble, though. No big surprise there. School teachers with college degrees did not normally wander into town, looking to hire on as ranch hands.

"I appreciate you taking the time to speak with me, sir." Since it didn't sound like Mr. Britt would be forthcoming with any more details about Bella's background, Asher had no reason to keep him on the phone.

"Just hope she lasts longer at your place than she did at mine."

"That makes two of us, sir."

The aging farmer was silent for a moment. Then he added in a wistful note, "I'd appreciate some assurance that you're gonna look after her better than I did."

Asher wasn't entirely sure what the man was talking about, but it probably wouldn't have changed his answer if he did. "I give you my word, sir."

He ended the call and sat there staring at Bella's other two job references. Normally, he called every one of them for a prospective candidate, but he'd heard all he needed to know from Mr. Britt. He had no doubt her background check would prove she'd served as a school teacher for three years in Dallas, the same city where her troubles had likely originated. And until he was better versed on them, it was probably best not to poke that cobra. If anything, it might alert the wrong person about her current whereabouts. So long as her background check and drug screening came back clean, he didn't mind bringing her on board.

It was probably crass of him to think this way, but he liked the idea of hiring a woman who needed money badly enough to put up with his cranky self, scars and all.

————

After warming up and getting clean in the shower, Bella spent the last half hour drying her hair and boots. The hair dryer she found under the sink made short work of her hair. Her boots, however, were another story. It was probably going to take days to finish drying them out. *Rain, rain, go away!* She was quickly discovering how erratic the weather could be up here in the Texas panhandle — icy cold one day and swimsuit weather the next, dry as a bone one evening followed by a deluge the next morning. Golly, but it was going to take some time to get used to it, time she may not have before being forced to move on to the next adventure. Her ex had been unusually persistent in tracking her down the entire year she'd been on the move, making her wonder if she should just sign off on the papers he kept waving under her nose and be done with him. He owed her a hefty chunk of change, though, from the house they'd purchased together. She hated letting him win that easily.

So she continued to scrimp and save, hoping she would eventually have the funds to afford a lawyer. She'd long since given up on the hope that her ex would return her money out of the goodness of his heart. She was no longer even sure he possessed a heart.

Opening doors and drawers, she gave a yelp of delight to discover a stacked washer and dryer behind a folding door in the bathroom, along with a few sample-sized packs of detergent. She quickly tossed her wet clothing in it and started a load. A wardrobe as small as hers required constant laundering. However, it made no sense to travel with an army of suitcases. It was easier to donate all the non-essentials to charity each time she hit the road and buy new stuff when she arrived at her next destination. Or gently used items, in her case, since she preferred to shop at yard sales and second-hand shops.

She found herself taking more care than usual as she dressed and braided her hair. Asher Cassidy was, hands down, the youngest boss she'd encountered since leaving Dallas. And the handsomest. And a thousand shades of hot. And most likely single, to boot — not that she was in the market for another boyfriend. *No thank you!* Still, it was way too bad to see the chip on his shoulder about his scars. In her humble opinion, they only ratcheted up his brooding appeal. Though he didn't see it that way now, hopefully he would see it someday, maybe when the right girl finally came along.

So not my business! Forcing her thoughts back to more professional ones about the man she would soon be reporting to, Bella bent closer to the mirror over the vanity to powder her nose. Then she added a layer of her favorite lip gloss. The sparkle on her lower lip inevitably made her mind drift back to the memory of Asher Cassidy's steely arms and hard mouth. After being thrown into his embrace earlier, she'd gotten a pretty close look at him. Close enough to verify that no part of his mouth was scarred, unlike the left side of his face. When he kissed a woman, there would be no puckered skin to distract from the moment. Once she closed her eyes, there would be nothing but the feel of his warm lips against hers.

Oh, my gosh! Just stop. The crazy direction of her thoughts made her wonder if she was more tired than she realized. Either that, or being chilled to the bone earlier had addled her brains. Whatever the case, it was time for her to stop daydreaming about stuff that was never going to happen. She needed to put on her game face.

Before closing the door of the loft apartment, she threw one last glance over her shoulder. She'd left her guitar case resting beside the black leather chair. It looked at home there, which made her heart give a tiny wrench of longing. Someday she was finally going to outrun her heartache and be ready to turn over a new leaf. Someday she was going to settle in and stay a while. Someday she was going to belong somewhere. Lord willing, someday.

Her gaze landed on Asher's rain jacket that she'd left tossed on the back of one of the stools. *Eep! Better return it.* She moved across the room to snatch it up. After a moment's hesitation, she shrugged it over her pale pink t-shirt instead of carrying it. She might as well enjoy its warmth a little longer. Plus, it would keep her shirt from getting soaked again outside.

She shut and locked the door behind her, then shot a quick glance at her watch. It was a mere two minutes shy of the time she'd agreed to meet up again with Asher. She might make it back in time if she ran.

Jogging down the stairs to the main floor of the horse barn, she was enchanted by the rows of lovely horses nickering in their stalls on both sides of the aisle. Two stories above her head, the rain beat a steady tempo on the metal roof. It was a wonderfully peaceful sound.

"Oh, you beautiful things," she sighed, pausing beside the stall closest to the stairs.

Behind the gate, a reddish-brown mare pawed impatiently at the ground, probably tired of being cooped up inside during such a long stint of rain. Unable to resist, Bella climbed on the lowest rung of the gate and held out a hand. "Hey there. What's your name?"

"Speed of Light," a male voice supplied.

Whipping her head around, Bella's gaze landed on the owner of the dog who'd plowed over her earlier. "She's pretty fast, huh?"

"Yup. She and I are the reigning cattle roping champs in the area." The cowboy swaggered her way with a hand outstretched. "I'm Fox Cassidy."

She hopped down from her perch to shake his hand. So Asher had been yelling at his own brother earlier. Or cousin.

Fox's Stetson was missing, but there was a line around his hair where it had been sitting. She wasn't surprised to learn he shared Asher Cassidy's last name. Their resemblance to each other was undeniable. Though Fox's face was free of scars, they had the same angular features and the same shade of brown hair, albeit Fox wore his a little longer. His black cherry colored ostrich skin boots were every bit as expensive looking, too, and his jeans — though fashionably frayed at the hem — were certainly no knock-off brand like hers.

"And you are?" A swatch of dark hair fell over the cowboy's eyes. He shoved it back to peer at her with unmistakable male curiosity. His gaze lingered a few seconds on the oversized jacket hanging halfway down her thighs.

"I'm Bella Johnson." When he seemed in no terrible hurry to let go of her hand, she gently disengaged it and returned it to her side. "The new ranch hand." And part-time personal assistant to the ranch manager.

"Finally!" Fox gave an exaggerated sigh of relief. "I put my order in for help months ago, but my oldest brother is as slow as molasses about stuff like that." He rolled his eyes. "Always harping about needing more time to get the right folks in the right places so we can keep the family feel of the place." He lifted his hands in the air to mockingly form air quotes around the words *family feel*.

Aha. So, her first guess was correct. They were brothers. No big surprise there. She nodded at his words despite the new questions they raised. For a guy who supposedly moved as slow as molasses on hiring decisions, Asher Cassidy had been mighty quick to offer her a job this morning. She couldn't help wondering why. What was it about her some-what harum-scarum resume that had made him decide she'd fit into a big family operation like theirs?

Then again, Asher's job offer wasn't exactly cemented in stone. He'd made it all too clear that it hinged directly on her references checking out, and she wasn't nearly as confident about that happening as she'd pretended to him. Old Eli Britt had been pretty mad about the ultra short notice she'd given him. However, he didn't have a dishonest bone in his body, so he'd at least tell Asher the truth about her work ethic. *I hope.* If not, she'd be job hunting again, possibly before nightfall.

Another glance at her watch revealed that her two

minutes of wiggle room were used up and then some. "Ah, snap!" She was running nearly five minutes late now. "I've gotta run. It was nice to meet you, Fox."

As she jogged down the plank hallway, Fox called after her, "You gonna be staying upstairs like the other ranch hands?"

"If my references check out," she tossed over her shoulder. *Please, Lord, let them check out. I need this job.* Pushing open the door, she dashed back out into the rain. Head down, she quickly traversed the short sidewalk and cut across the grassy lawn.

Almost immediately upon leaving the sidewalk, she slammed into a hard wall of flesh. *Not again!* Giving an oomph of surprise, Bella grabbed two handfuls of the person's shirt, wondering who she'd plowed into this time. However, their speed of impact proved too much for the rain-slicked grass. Before she could identify her latest victim, they slipped and slid together to the ground.

"I'm so sorry!" she gasped, scrambling as quickly as she could from the chest of the man she'd pinned to the grass. Her hands and knees landed on the damp ground, quickly soaking through the legs of her fresh pair of jeans.

"We seem to be making a habit of this." Asher's husky baritone filled her ears, making her heart pitch in dismay.

"I'm so sorry," she babbled again. "I'm not normally this-this…" She struggled for the right word, mortified beyond belief at having so gracelessly collided with her prospective boss twice in the same morning.

The amount of mud and rain on his jeans made her stomach turn queasy, almost certain that he was going to fire her on the spot.

His expression was impossible to read as he rolled forward to his feet and extended a hand to her. "I swear this is the last time I'm going to wear a new pair of boots to work."

She felt the color drain from her face. "If they're damaged, I'll pay for them." Eventually. After she received her next paycheck, which may or may not come from Cassidy Farm, considering how bad her first day was going.

"They'll clean up," he assured dryly. "I just meant they're not broken in yet, which is the only reason a woman the size of a firefly has managed to knock me off my feet twice."

"A firefly?" She chuckled, even though there was nothing funny about their situation. "No one has ever called me that before."

The rain abruptly stopped, leaving them staring at each other through drenched eyelashes. He was a man of average height, only topping her petite frame by two or three inches. A lot of guys towered a lot higher over her, so it was kind of nice that he didn't.

With his blue and white plaid shirt as damp as her own, she was able to see how bone-thin he was. Too thin, as if he'd recently been ill. It was probably the real reason she'd been able to knock him over so easily. Her guilt increased at the haunted cast to his blue gaze that was probing hers.

"I really am sorry," she murmured again, at a loss for what else to say.

He snorted. "It's a farm, Bella. If I couldn't handle a little mud and muck, I'd get a different job."

She let out a silent exhale of relief. It didn't sound like he'd hunted her down to fire her, at least not yet. "About that paperwork I was supposed to fill out…"

"It'll wait." His voice was dry again. "Since we're both as filthy as farm animals, we might as well make our first round of the livestock now."

Their first round, as it turned out, was far more than a tour. Unrolling hoses, they refilled the galvanized steel watering troughs for the cattle in the pasture behind the barn. Next, he showed her the hay barn and had her tote a few bales back to the horses.

Despite his gauntness, he was able to carry twice as many at a time as she could. *Show off!* No stranger to farm chores, however, she worked quickly and efficiently.

His expression registered grudging approval as they finished feeding and watering all eight of the horses. "On days when Fox is off riding the rodeo circuit, you'll need to help care for the horses."

"No problem." She nodded. "I passed him in the barn on my way outside, and he stopped to introduce himself. Sounds like he has quite a title to ˙ˉᶠᵉnd."

wo or three." The bleak twist to Asher's hard

mouth made her wonder if he ever smiled. He abruptly changed the subject. "By the way, my mother serves lunch at noon sharp Monday through Saturday. She expects the ranch hands to join us."

"Wow! Thanks!" Bella was surprised to hear it. "How many of us ranch hands are there?"

"Three, counting you."

It didn't sound like many employees for such a big farming operation.

"She takes Sundays off, but she sets out a continental breakfast the night before. You'll see what I'm talking about soon enough."

Since it was only Monday, Bella blinked at the realization that Asher Cassidy expected her to last that long, everything considered. "Wow!" she said again. "That's fantastic." To save money, she often went down to one meal per day, but it didn't sound like food was going to be a problem here at Cassidy Farm. A cautious ribbon of hope unfurled inside her.

Asher strode across the pasture, forcing her to kick it in gear to catch up with him. Glancing at her watch, she was surprised to discover it was a few minutes shy of noon already.

Her stomach gave a growl of hunger at the reminder it had been nearly twenty-four hours since her last meal. "Lovely," she muttered, pressing a hand to her midsection. Even on days when she ate breakfast, farm chores always made her work up an appetite.

Though Asher spared her a curious glance, he didn't say anything. As they trudged past a pair of log cabins to the main ranch house, Bella inwardly bemoaned how filthy she was. Her only comfort was that the mid-morning breezes had finished drying the dampness from her clothing. The temperature was a good ten to fifteen degrees warmer than it had been during the rainstorm. All in all, it was turning out to be a pleasant day, despite its soggy beginning.

Since they were heading that way, she could only presume that the meals Asher had been talking about would be served at his parents' place. Did he live there as well? He seemed a little old to still be living at home, but what did she know about the dynamics of big families?

The sprawling ranch home was set atop a small hill, which she imagined gave the occupants a bird's-eye-view of the entire ranch. *Lucky dogs!* If she had the good fortune to live in such luxury, she'd never miss another sunrise. She could only imagine how breathtaking the distant canyons appeared at first light from such a vantage point.

It was one of those rambling type houses that had probably been added on to several times. The second floor was only a half-story, but it boasted dormer windows that extended the space and gave whoever lived up there the best view of the entire property. The exterior walls were stucco, freshly painted a shade of whipped cream. In recent months, she'd discovered that a lot of folks in the southwest painted their homes that color to deflect the heat of the sun.

The windows of the home were offset by stained wooden shutters that matched the front door. A country lantern hung directly over the door, and a spacious veranda stretched along the entire front of the house. Craftsman columns and stained oak rockers completed the cozy, inviting setting.

Asher jogged up the steps ahead of Bella to hold open the door for her. As usual, he was unsmiling, and his expression gave away nothing. However, she took heart in the kindness of his gesture. He might not be a warm and fuzzy kind of guy, but he possessed good old-fashioned manners. That was worth something in her book. Her ex-fiancé had never been in the position to extend those kinds of courtesies to her. He hadn't been allowed to publicly acknowledge their relationship at all — a fact she'd realized in hindsight had been all too convenient for the double life he'd chosen to lead. Since he served as the principal of the high school where she'd taught, they'd been forced to date on the sly. And become engaged on the sly. The plan had been for them to marry on the sly, too, right up until she'd discovered he'd been cheating on her with one of the English teachers.

"You coming inside or what?" Asher's harsh voice jolted Bella out of the fog of melancholy settling over her.

Nodding, she quickly stepped past him across the threshold. An enormous braided rug took up most of the entry foyer. A bench rested on one side, just below the stairs. A pile of books rested on one end of it, and a quilt was draped across the opposite arm. To their right was a living room with a wall of bookcases for a backdrop. Bella gave the baby grand piano a longing look. There'd been an upright piano at her grandparents' home, where she'd spent many hours picking out songs by ear. As an adult, she'd taught herself how to play the guitar. It was a much cheaper instrument to purchase, and it was hundreds of pounds lighter to carry around. If she ever got the opportunity, though, she wouldn't think twice about running her fingers over the ivories again.

Swallowing a sigh of nostalgia, she transferred her attention to the other side of the entry foyer. Beyond the stairs leading to the second story was a pair of glass paneled doors that had been propped open. Behind them was the dining room. Since several people were already seated around a long farmhouse table spanning the length of the room, she could only presume this was where they were supposed to have lunch.

Most of the room's occupants were men. Several of the younger ones resembled Asher. So did the oldest one at the head of the table. She knew without asking that he must be the senior Mr. Cassidy, Asher's father. He didn't look old enough to be a grandfather. Two of the younger guys resembled Asher's mother. Bella blinked at the realization they were identical twins. *Twins! How cool is that?*

There was only one other female in the room besides Bella and Mrs. Cassidy, and she didn't resemble the Cassidys one bit. The moment Asher's gaze fell on her, he visibly stiffened.

"Jade," he said in such a cold voice that Bella's heart ached for him.

"Asher," the woman answered softly. "It's been a long time, hasn't it? Too long."

An awkward silence settled over the room as the tension between the two of them escalated to nearly excruciating levels. Or that's what it felt like to Bella.

She couldn't help staring at the woman. Jade's strawberry blonde hair cascaded around delicate-looking shoulders that were encased in a silk aquamarine blouse. She possessed a milky complexion that often came with redheads, minus the sprinkling of freckles that just as often accompanied such a hair color. In short, she was perfect.

Just being in the same room as her made Bella feel wind blown, sunburnt, and filthy.

"Bella," Mrs. Cassidy announced brightly, waving at the empty seat between her and Jade. "Please join us. Jade, this is our new ranch hand, Bella Johnson. Bella, this is a long-time friend of the family, Jade Arletta."

The young woman gave Bella a tight, assessing smile that seemed to take in everything from her tousled appearance to the oversized jacket she'd all but forgotten she was still wearing. "Like the Cassidys, the Arlettas are one of the founding families of our town," she announced in a lofty voice, "which is why I've been given the task of organizing Chipper's first official hoedown."

"A hoedown?" Asher snorted as he took the last empty seat at the table. It was directly across from the one where Jade sat. "Are you sure Chipper has a big enough population to justify a hoedown?"

"Of course we do," Jade snapped. "Our last census put us at twelve hundred and thirty-five citizens."

He shrugged and reached for the glass of tea his mother had just poured for him. "Still not sure you'll have many attendees since it's planting season." He couldn't have sounded more bored or disinterested in the event.

"Which is why I'm paying every family a visit to extend a personal invitation." Jade tossed her head. "It's going to take events like this to fundraise that fire department into existence that your mother is campaigning so hard for."

Bella watched as Asher's gaze flickered to the woman in question. "Seems to me we can just as easily make a donation toward the cause and be done with it."

"And how would that unify our new town and make us feel part of something?" Jade fumed. "I say we can do better than that."

"What all do you have in mind for the hoedown, dear?" Mrs. Cassidy interjected quickly after a glance of concern between the two of them.

Jade's red-painted lips curved into a smug smile. "For one thing, I'm recruiting grill masters for a BBQ cook-off. We'll charge per entry and per plate. Not only will it raise money, it'll allow someone to go home with bragging rights. I can think of a few cocky cowboys right off the bat who won't be able to resist such a challenge." She fluttered her lashes in Asher's direction. "I'll also be looking for volunteers for the kissing booth."

Kissing booth! Bella, who'd been reaching for her tea glass, glanced up in surprise. As a result, she missed the glass she'd intended to pick up, grazing the side of it instead. She watched in horror as it tipped in Jade's direction.

The world seemed to skid into slow motion as the brown liquid gushed from the overturned glass and splashed across the table.

"Oh, no!" Bella moaned, diving for her napkin. *What is wrong with me?* She'd always been a bit of a klutz, but today she seemed bent on setting new records. She frantically held out her napkin to the gasping, spluttering woman beside her. "I'm so sorry," she breathed. Every eye in the room was on her. She wanted to expire from mortification.

CHAPTER 3:
BARGAINING WITH THE ENEMY

ASHER

ASHER COULDN'T REMEMBER the last time he'd felt this much like laughing. He was pretty sure it was before the fire that had nearly ended his life, and he was very sure it was before the accident-prone Bella Johnson had stumbled her way into his world. The petite cowgirl had proven to be a demon worker when it came to farm chores, but she was otherwise a walking, talking calamity. The agonized look staining her face told him that she was all too aware of that fact.

Her tanned cheeks were mottled at least three different shades of red beneath her sprinkling of freckles, and she looked ready to bolt from the room. If only she had a clue how satisfying it was for him to witness Jade frantically dabbing at the tea stains on the silk fabric of her blouse — a blouse he was willing to bet she cared more about than him back when they were dating.

"I'll pay to have it drycleaned," Bella assured breathlessly.

"It's probably ruined," Jade snapped.

"Then I'll replace it."

"I highly doubt that, since it's one-of-a-kind from Venice."

At Bella's blank look, Jade added, "I bought it during my last trip to Italy."

"Oh!" Bella's red cheeks suddenly waxed pale. She looked so close to fainting that Asher knew it was time to intervene.

"Since Bella is our employee, Cassidy Farm will take responsibility for any damage to your shirt, Jade."

She abruptly stood, making her chair scrape harshly against the tile floor. Fox, who was sitting on the other side of her, winced and reached over to slide the chair back a few more inches. "I sure hope you have two thousand dollars handy," she seethed through gritted teeth.

Ouch! That's a pretty penny. Asher raised his brows at her, wondering if she was exaggerating just to be nasty. In the past, she'd been prone to dramatic outbursts when she was angry.

"Do you think I'm kidding?" she spat. "Because I can send you the receipt if you'd like."

"That won't be necessary," he growled. "Just tell us what we need to do to make this right." *Even better, what can we do to make you go away?*

"I'll resign," Bella babbled in a shaky voice. "I'll go pack my things right now." She stood so quickly that she knocked over her chair. Again, Fox's lightning quick reflexes saved the day.

Asher felt his lips twitch, wondering what their newest employee was talking about since she literally had nothing to pack. "Meet me in my office, Bella," he instructed. He stood to glare across the table at Jade. "Well?"

"As a matter-of-fact, there is something you can do to make amends." She tilted her chin up haughtily.

Here it comes. When she didn't immediately enlighten the occupants of the room about her wishes, Asher impatiently waved at her to continue. "We're listening."

"All six of you Cassidy brothers can consider yourselves signed up for the kissing booth at the hoedown."

"Whoa!" Beldon half-rose from his seat, raising his hands in protest. The look he shot her had a surprising element of warning in it. "Shouldn't we discuss this first?"

Their mother broke into a tinkling laugh. "What's there to talk about? It sounds like a fair trade to me." She sought out her husband's gaze.

To Asher's alarm, Ridge Cassidy nodded in agreement, running a callused hand through his hair. The gesture ruffled the strands at his temples. He was grinning as widely as his wife was, which made no sense to Asher. For the life of him, he couldn't see anything funny about the situation. Neither could his brothers, from the looks on their faces. Their expressions ranged from aghast to infuriated, except for Beldon. His face was impossible to read.

"If it was me, I'd fork over a few kisses any day to save two thousand dollars," their father continued in a mild voice. "Shoot! When I was young and single, I didn't need a reason. I'd do it just because." He sent a heated look down the table at his wife.

Asher stared at him in disbelief. *Whose side are you on?* It was Jade Arletta they were talking about here. Who cared if she ended up with a permanent tea stain on one of her precious shirts? It was no less than the hard-hearted woman deserved, and everyone around the table knew it.

Claire Cassidy spread her hands innocently, sending a beseeching look around the table at her sons. "It's for a good cause," she reminded them sweetly. "Besides, everyone knows I have the handsomest, most kissable sons in town."

Fox made a few gagging sounds and pretended to storm from the room. "I'm outta here," he announced to no one in particular. "Think I've got a few granola bars stashed in the barn." As much as Fox loved to eat, his message was clear. He'd rather starve than spend another minute in Jade's presence.

Claire Cassidy rolled her eyes at his retreating shoulder blades. "Just think of how much equipment your kisses will buy and how many lives they might save, son," she called after him.

He plugged his fingers into his ears and kept walking.

She shook her head at him, chuckling. "Oh, come

on! What's a few kisses to a few single fellas like you?"

"Nothing," Devlin waved a hand airily. "That's kind of the point. I think I speak for us all when I say none of us are interested in handing out a bunch of meaningless kisses, not even for a good cause." He and his twin, Emerson, were the only two brothers who'd inherited her blonde hair. The other four brothers had their father's shade of brown. At least, that was the color it used to be before the frost that now speckled his sideburns. "Surely, there's a better way to raise money for the fire department."

Asher knew exactly what his younger brother meant. In a small town like theirs, with so few available bachelors, single ladies could read an awful lot into a few kisses. The last woman Devlin dated had broken up in a tizzy when he'd failed to propose six or seven weeks into their relationship.

"Then who should I send the bill for my shirt to?" Jade shot a furious look in Bella's direction.

The Cassidy's new ranch hand swayed on her feet, looking ready to faint.

Watching her, Asher answered in a mechanical voice, "You can send it to me."

"What?" Beldon exploded, staring at him like he'd lost his mind.

"I don't know, Ash." Devlin's expression was much the same as Beldon's.

"Unless anyone else in the room has two thousand dollars to spend on Italian silk..." Asher shrugged dispassionately. As far as he was concerned, the subject was closed.

"I was referring to the kissing booth," Devlin hastened to explain. "Like Dad said, maybe we should reconsider."

"I'll, ah… If you'll please excuse me." Bella took a stumbling step toward the door.

Asher jerked his head toward the barn that housed their administrative offices. "I'll meet you back at the office in five."

She all but dashed from the room. By some miracle, she made it out the front door without knocking anything else over.

Ignoring Jade, Asher circled the table to bend and speak in his Mother's ear. "Got any to-go boxes?" Recalling the way Bella's stomach had rumbled, he figured it had been a long time since her last meal. He needed her fit for farm work, not fainting from hunger.

"You know I do," his mother answered softly. "Take a look in the cabinet below the island."

He nodded and made his way to the kitchen without looking back. Instead of returning to the dining room to scoop up ham and mashed potatoes from the feast displayed on the table, he opened his parents' new stainless steel refrigerator to see what else there was to eat. His mother had an array of cold-cuts laid out on a wide silver tray beneath a layer of cellophane, probably for later that evening. Hoping she'd forgive him for digging into them early, he quickly assembled a small pile of sandwiches and tossed them inside the to-go boxes. Instead of retracing his steps through the dining room or hallway, he exited out the side door from the kitchen.

He sincerely hoped he'd find Bella waiting for him in his office when he got there. He didn't know what it was about the woman, only that her deer-in-the-headlights response to Jade's treatment had tugged at his deepest sympathies. In Jade's presence, Bella's toughness from earlier had all but disappeared. She'd transformed into a cowed, beaten-down version of her former self. Asher had every intention of finding out why and getting back the woman he'd hired.

Marching into the administrative building, he found his office door ajar. That was a good sign. Pushing it open, he found Bella standing at the far window, staring outside with her arms wrapped tightly around her middle.

"I can't do this," she mumbled the moment he stepped inside the room. "I thought I could, but I can't. I meant what I said about submitting my resignation."

"Request denied." He stepped farther into the room.

· She spun around, looking amazed. "You can't do that."

He shrugged. "The way I see it, you owe Cassidy Farm two thousand dollars. Seems to me the only decent thing you can do is stay and work it off." He had no intention of charging her for the funds, but it was the only thing he could think of to say that might keep her from marching straight out of the door and out of his life.

"I-I..." She stuttered to a halt.

"I'm kidding," he assured dryly. Marching across the room, he deposited the to-go boxes on his desk. "I brought some sandwiches from the kitchen."

"I'm no longer hungry," she informed him stiffly. A half-second later, her stomach growled again, more loudly than before.

"Liar," he accused.

"Fine. You got me. I'm hungry," she sighed. "I'm still not going to eat. I'm not going to come anywhere near you until you produce whatever paperwork I need to sign to terminate my position here. I really do think it's best if I leave."

And go where? "My ex really got to you, didn't she?"

When Bella didn't answer, he opened one of the food boxes, withdrew a sandwich, and carried it across the room to her. He was probably breaking every standard of etiquette by holding it with his bare hand, but he was past caring about the rules. "Here. Choke it down if you have to, but you worked like a dog all morning. You need to eat."

She angrily swiped the sandwich from his hand despite her previous protests about not wanting to eat. "Why do you care?"

"Because you work for me now. In case you haven't noticed the piles of paperwork on my desk, I am in desperate need of some assistance."

Her hand shook as she held the sandwich, tugging his sympathies all over again. "You sure you want to take a chance on me? I seem to only be capable of dropping things, tripping over stuff, and falling into people today."

"Yeah, I noticed." He had a bruised backside to prove it.

"I honestly don't know what's wrong with me."

"Nothing's wrong with you." Except exhaustion, maybe. As the day wore on, the purplish shadows under her eyes grew more pronounced. "And, yes. For the umpteenth time, I'm sure about hiring you. Come on over and take a seat." Not waiting for her to comply, he took a seat behind his desk.

"Have you called my references yet?" She spun around to scowl at him.

"Only one of them, so far. I talked to Eli Britt earlier."

"Oh?" She swayed dizzily.

"Please. Sit down." He pointed at the pair of chairs across from his desk, genuinely concerned that she was about to pass out. "You're putting a crick in my neck over there."

She moved silently across the room and, more or less, collapsed into the nearest upholstered chair. "I'm sorry about what happened in the dining room."

"Quit apologizing."

"I mean it," she insisted.

"I honestly haven't enjoyed myself that much in a year," he informed her flatly.

"I'm glad you find my misery so amusing."

"Not yours. Hers." He snickered.

Bella's lush mouth fell open. "Did you just laugh?"

"I'm not sure. I'm a little rusty at it," he joked. "Did it sound like a laugh to you?"

She shrugged. "I'm trying to decide if that's a good thing, considering how I seem to be the source of your amusement."

"Thank you."

"You're not welcome," she retorted sourly and finally took a bite of the sandwich. She made a humming sound in the back of her throat. "Omigosh! This is so good."

Man! She was beautiful. Asher studied his dusty, famished new employee with growing wonder as she devoured her sandwich, eyes closed. For the first time in months, his scars were the furthest thing from his mind. When Bella was in the room — heck, make that anywhere in the vicinity! — he was too busy being distracted, entertained, or otherwise enchanted. She was one of those people who seemed to soak up every moment. She was so alive. So real. So genuine, flaws and all. Being around her felt like taking a long and satisfying drag of sweet, fresh air.

Only after she polished off her sandwich did she open her eyes. "If you agree to bring me on board, I'm going to owe you big-time for the whole kissing booth thing."

"I already brought you on board," he reminded.

She continued as if she hadn't heard, "And I think

we both know I'm not in the position to come up with two thousand dollars."

"Not doing the kissing booth."

"You will if the rest of your family out-votes you, which they seem inclined to do."

"If it makes you feel better, consider yourself in possession of an IOU."

"I'm serious, Asher."

"So am I."

"What can I do to square us up? For real?"

"I'll think of something. And if you're right about being strong-armed into working the kissing booth, I'll be facing complete and utter humiliation."

She scowled. "What do you mean?"

He pointed at his damaged face, surprised that she needed an explanation. "This mug isn't exactly a money maker these days."

"Oh, please!" she snapped. "Women love the dark, broody look."

He arched one eyebrow at her. "Did you just call me cranky?"

"Maybe." She snickered. "Sorry. I seem to have misplaced my nice girl filter today. Guess I've been out of the classroom too long. Add it to my long list of flaws."

He grimaced. "Well, that's some fine writing for you. Wait until after I hire you to give me the full low-down on what I'm getting into."

"Do you really mean it about keeping me on board?" She spread her hands, looking so deliciously wind-tousled and uncertain that he found it impossible to tear his gaze away from her. "After all my klutziness, inappropriate laughter, and everything else I'm bound to botch up?"

"I already answered that question. Next issue." He waved again at the piles of paperwork on his desk. "How long do you think it will take you to work through a few dozen address changes? Cassidy Farm is in dire need of having its vendors informed of our new location."

She wrinkled her nose at him. "Why the address change? I thought your mother said this place has been in your family for generations."

"Did she also happen to mention winning her petition to incorporate our small farming community into the new township of Chipper?"

"Uh…no."

"Well, that's how you change your address without moving an inch. Thank you, Mom."

She leaned forward in her chair to fiddle with the nearest stack of forms. "This doesn't exactly require a college degree. All I'm looking at is a few hours of boring, tedious work."

"Still wondering why I hired you?" he countered.

Her pink lips curved upward. "I'm beginning to get the idea."

"Well, have at it." He glanced around the office. "Since it's going to take a few days, I'll probably cart an extra desk up here for you.

She nodded, looking thoughtful. "So, a few dozen change of address forms will square us up?"

"It'll help." Man, but he was desperate for an

extra set of hands in the office! The many upgrades his parents had made in recent months at Cassidy Farm had attracted a decent amount of press. Thanks to a feature on a major television network, they now had customers driving thirty to forty-five minutes each week to shop their meats, produce, canned goods, and homemade soaps and candles. It was all he could do to keep their inventory logs balanced and their pricing strategies current while still keeping the family feel of the place intact. They'd built a solid reputation on that last item that Asher never intended to give up. He was grateful for their sudden burst of increased business, but he was quickly learning that every growth spurt came with its own set of growing pains. Only time would tell if Bella Johnson was going to be part of the solution or part of the growing pains.

His shoulders tensed as he leaned his forearms on his desk. "In the spirit of full disclosure, I spoke to Eli Britt before lunch."

"And?" She seemed to be holding her breath.

"Like you said, the reference checked out."

She let out a silent sigh. "Another hurdle crossed."

"Not quite. He was pretty hacked about you leaving." He lifted his cell phone in the air and waved it suggestively at her.

Her face fell. "I'm as sorry as I can be about the short notice I gave him."

"Sorry isn't going to cut it this time." Asher slid his phone across the desk between two stacks of paper. "He's expecting a phone call from you right about now."

"What's the point?" She stared at the phone as if it were a snake. "Nothing I say is ever going to make him forgive me."

"Actually, all he wants is to make sure I'm who I say I am before he mails your last paycheck to this address."

"Are you serious?" She pressed a hand to her chest.

"Not all men are monsters, Bella." He glanced away. "Even though some of us may look like it."

"I wish you'd stop saying stuff like that."

He watched out of the corner of his eye as she mechanically reached for his phone. "If the shoe fits," he muttered.

"Oh, for crying out loud!" she exploded. "If I wasn't flat broke, I'd jump into the kissing booth line myself and plant one on you just to prove how wrong you are."

His heart leaped at the vehemence in her voice. It made him wonder if there was some hope left for him, after all, in the romance department. Though the puckers in his skin would never entirely disappear, the brilliance of the scars was fast fading to fainter hues of pink and silver.

Watching his rapidly changing expression, she turned the most fascinating shade of crimson. "Omigosh! Missing filter again. What I was trying to say was—"

"Relax," he cut in. "No red-blooded male in Texas

would complain if you kissed him. Myself included. With a little luck, someone would start the rumor that you and I are more than professionally involved, and everyone would finally stop feeling sorry for me."

"Seriously?" She stared at him. "If that's all you're worried about, we could skip the kiss that I can't afford and just pretend to be a couple."

Her offer intrigued him. "You really think you could fool my brothers?" It actually wasn't a half-bad idea.

"I don't think it. I *know* it." She lifted her chin. "I kind of hate to admit this, but you wouldn't be the first boss I've dated. It didn't work out in the end, but..." Her voice dwindled into silence.

Interesting. For reasons he didn't care to delve too closely into right now, Asher was glad to hear that things hadn't worked out with Bella's ex. The bitterness in her voice, however, told him he might've accidentally stumbled on the real reason why she'd left her teaching job.

"Yeah, well, if we agree to do this, it'll be different this time since we'd only be fake dating. No commitments required." He watched her closely for her reaction, wondering if she was serious about the offer.

"True." Her expression brightened. "And when the ladies line up to kiss you at the hoedown, you can fake break up with me and finally move on with your life."

"Move on?" he repeated.

"It's clear you still have feelings for your ex."

"It is?" It wasn't true, of course, but he was curious about what had given Bella that impression.

"No? My bad. I guess I just assumed that's what all your crabbing was about."

He grunted. "I'm not still hung up on my ex. I was only trying to explain why I don't expect to get much action at the kissing booth."

She shrugged. "I'm not sure I agree. That said, anyone who has a problem with the way you look isn't worth kissing, anyway."

"You're right. She wasn't." He shook his head. "She dumped me the moment life threw us our first curve ball."

Bella nodded. "Like I said during my interview, things happen for a reason. And sometimes they don't...for a reason."

Their gazes locked for a moment, and awareness prickled between them. He was the first to speak again. "Like that phone call that's never gonna happen if you don't start dialing?" he teased, pointing at the phone she was still clutching.

"Right." She tapped the screen to turn it on.

"It's the last call I made. Just hit redial."

She paused before complying. "How mad was he?"

"Didn't peg you for a coward, Bella."

"You don't know anything about me, Asher."

"We might have to agree to disagree on that point." His voice was teasing. "I have the bruises on my sitter to prove we're pretty well acquainted by now."

Her expression twisted with remorse all over again. "I'm so sorry!" She sat back in her chair, looking miserably deflated.

"Prove it," he taunted, waving at his desk. "After your call of shame to Mr. Britt, there should be plenty of time left to get started on those pesky change of address forms."

"I change my mind about what I said earlier," she muttered, finally punching the re-dial button. "You really are a monster."

"And I'm just getting started," he assured silkily. "You ain't seen nothin' yet, cowgirl."

CHAPTER 4: FAKE GIRLFRIEND

BELLA

ASHER HADN'T BEEN KIDDING when he warned Bella about being a tough taskmaster. The next two weeks passed in a blur of farm chores, a maniacal amount of paperwork, and no small amount of planning for the upcoming hoedown. It was to take place in the newly constructed stadium on Saturday, and everyone in the Cassidy family had a role to play.

Claire and Ridge would be unveiling a concrete statue in the likeness of Chipper Cassidy to transport and mount at the park surrounding Town Square. The twins were participating in the chili cook-off, Fox was riding in the midday parade, and all six brothers would be staffing the kissing booth in the afternoon. Jade had been unclear about whether there would be any other cowboys joining them, or if she'd reserved the kissing booth as their special punishment for her ruined shirt.

Asher stomped into the room Friday morning, looking thunderous.

"Now what?" Bella sighed, sensing trouble. She'd risen an hour early to beat him to the office in the hopes of finishing the last set of address changes. It had been every bit as long and laborious of a project as she'd imagined it would be, and it hadn't been easy fitting it in around all of her other responsibilities.

"I just overheard a conversation between my parents that I wish I could un-hear," he snarled without preamble.

She straightened a stack of folders and glanced up expectantly.

"I have reason to think they're trying to get me and Jade Arletta back together."

"No way!" Though Bella was the newest employee at the ranch, she'd been there long enough to know that sounded nothing like his kindhearted parents.

"Then explain their intentions to march every single lady in Chipper through the kissing booth. That'll include Jade, you know. And there's no way they didn't have a hand in putting her in charge of the event in the first place. My parents are behind every major decision that's made in this blasted town."

Bella chuckled. "So they have plans to introduce their single sons to a few lovely ladies. Wanting to become grandparents someday doesn't make them bad people."

"Did you hear the part about them herding all the single ladies through the kissing booth?" he repeated in a peevish tone. "I checked just to be sure and verified that Jade is very much between boyfriends."

"Well, I'm not," Bella reminded, fluttering her lashes at him. "You're already spoken for, remember?"

"Am I?" He stalked to the window to stare outside. "The hoedown is tomorrow, and you and I still haven't made our first move to establish ourselves as a couple. Nobody's going to believe we're dating when all you've done is work from dawn until dusk since the day you arrived."

"And whose fault is that?" She didn't know whether to laugh or throw something at him. "I've literally been buried in work." Not that she was complaining. Asher paid her well for what she did.

"Which doesn't explain the long solo horse rides you take every evening or the number of dinners you skip," he pointed out testily.

She tossed her pen down on her desk. "Are you seriously complaining to your fake girlfriend about not pretending to spend more time with you?" Though they'd discussed the possibilities, she didn't recall them coming to any hard and fast decisions about following through with the fake couple thing.

He stalked back toward the small writing desk he'd hauled into his office thirteen days ago. "Yeah. I guess I am." He leaned both hands down on her desk to bring them eye to eye. "The hoedown is tomorrow," he repeated.

"So you keep saying." She couldn't help chuckling at the storm clouds gathering in his blue gaze.

"What's so funny?" He scowled at her.

"You. Us." She shrugged. "Keep griping at me like this, and everyone else will assume we eloped weeks ago."

He curled his upper lip at her. "Because?"

"Because you bicker like an old married couple, that's what." Fox swaggered into the room, hands jammed into the pockets of his jeans. As he came to stand beside Bella's desk, his head swiveled back and forth between them. "So, are you two dating or what?"

"No!" Bella snapped.

"Yes!" Asher bellowed at the same time.

Fox smirked past the dark lock of hair that had fallen over his eyes. "Pardon my confusion, but you don't seem to be on the same sheet there."

"What do you want?" Asher growled, straightening to his full height to transfer his glare to his youngest brother.

"I was just wondering when you two were going to admit what's really going on between you," Fox suggested with an impish grin. "You've been dancing around the issue for two straight weeks." He began to pace the room, casting an occasional shrewd glance in their direction.

Bella waved a finger triumphantly at Asher. "Told you I'd fool them."

"Oh, I see what's really going on here." Fox swaggered back in their direction. "I should have known, because Asher's way too grumpy for a guy who's been kissed recently, and you two don't spend any of your free time together."

"Exactly. That's my point." Asher wagged a finger accusingly at her.

"Because you only want the rest of us to *think* you're dating, though you're really not," Fox concluded in triumph.

Bella shot Asher a rueful look. "He's pretty clever."

"In a bratty sort of way. Don't give him too much credit."

Fox twirled his hat on one finger. "I can only presume this means you've gotten wind of our parents' matchmaking plans for us."

"Unfortunately." Asher shook his head while hitching a hip on the edge of Bella's desk.

"It also means you beat me to the only female employee on the farm and already arm-twisted her into helping you out. Must be nice," he huffed, "being in the position to hire your own work wife, while the rest of us are out there getting shot up on the front lines."

Asher's eyebrows rose. "Didn't you just return from a three-day hunting trip?"

"Where I bagged three wild turkeys to roast at the hoedown, my outstanding contribution to Devlin and Emerson's chili, yes. But that's beside the point."

"Is it?" Asher folded his arms.

"Yes, because you'll have the lovely Bella Johnson

on your arm tomorrow, while the rest of us are stuck kissing frogs."

Asher shot a questioning look at Bella. "I haven't gone public with our status as a fake couple, because I wasn't aware it was official."

She burst out laughing. "I seriously had no idea our fake relationship was waiting to be moved into an officially fake status."

His youngest brother snickered and jammed a thumb in her direction. "Wherever you found her, I want one."

Asher spread his hands. "I'm going to need a compelling reason to get out of the kissing booth. So, yes. Our fake relationship would need to be an offi-cially official one."

"Or," Fox suggested in a sly voice, "you could pay Bella under the table to buy out all of your kisses. I mean, aren't we supposed to be raising money for the fire department?"

"Out!" Asher pointed toward the door, glaring at him.

Fox ignored him. "So, what's it going to be, love-birds? An official fake relationship or an unofficial one?"

"Guess you'll find out tomorrow." Bella rested her chin on her hands as she shot Asher a curious look. She wished she knew what he really wanted from her. "Far be it from me to spoil the surprise," she added lightly, hoping neither brother would guess how much time in the last twenty-four hours she'd spent thinking about that exact topic. She'd daydreamed about kissing her moody boss way too many times lately.

Despite how much he was dreading the idea of serving in the kissing booth, she secretly hoped he didn't succeed in weaseling out of it. She planned to be the first in line. A week ago, she'd received Mr. Britt's paycheck in the mail. Plus, Asher had just this morning disbursed her first set of wages from Cassidy Farm. She could easily afford to gamble away both her dignity and his at the kissing booth tomorrow. Maybe — just maybe — it would help him finally get over his hang-up about his scars.

One thing was for sure, if she dared to do something so bold, there was only one Cassidy brother she was interested in kissing.

"How do you prefer to handle it?" Asher reached over to lightly tap her nose.

"Even I can't deny the kissing booth is for a good cause."

She swatted away his hand. "So everyone keeps saying."

"Because it is." He caught her hand in mid-air and raised it to his lips to press a light kiss on her knuckles.

She stared at him in surprise as the tender gesture sent a bolt of warmth and wonder straight to her heart.

"I don't know what the right answer is," she answered. Her voice held a breathless edge to it. "How do you want to handle it?"

"By laying proper groundwork for our fake relationship." He threaded his fingers through hers as he lowered their hands to her desk.

"Go big or go home, huh?" It was an effort to keep her voice normal at the warmth and pressure of their joined hands. She liked the twinkle her words brought to his eyes, though.

"Always. How about we head over to the diner after you exercise the horses? Half the town will be there. That should get the ball rolling."

Trying to sound as casual as he did, she retorted, "If you truly expect me to put on a dress for you tonight, you'd best drag your cranky self to the barn and help me out with the horses."

His gaze darkened with interest. "You own a dress? Since when?"

She flicked one braid over her shoulder. "I might have gone shopping the other day after Farmer Britt's check arrived."

"Huh!" He studied her curiously. "Will I even recognize you?"

"Ha ha." She shot him a withering look.

Fox drawled, "I really hope you don't expect me to keep such a juicy secret from Beldon and the other guys."

Bella's head jerked in his direction to find him lounging against the door frame, shaking his head in bemusement at them. She'd all but forgotten he was still in the office.

"I don't mind keeping our brothers in the loop." Asher gave him a warning look. "Just keep our meddling parents out of it, thank you very much."

"Deal, but my silence will cost you." Fox straightened, pushing away from the door frame.

"Thought you still owed me for the way Ghost tore through my office the other day."

Bella wasn't sure if Asher realized he was still holding her hand as he taunted his brother. However, she didn't mind. She liked the way his callused fingers felt against hers, gentle with an undeniable note of possessiveness. She bit back a sigh at the realization he was probably only practicing for their fake date later that evening.

"I cleaned up the mess, so that debt's already settled. No double dipping, bro."

"I'm not approving a vacation day for tomorrow," Asher shook his head, "so don't bother asking."

"I didn't."

"Good. Because the plan is for us Cassidys to suffer through the kissing booth together."

"Some more than others." Fox glanced pointedly down at their joined hands.

———

Bella was secretly tickled to death when Asher met her in the horse barn a half hour later. "You made it!" Her heart leaped at the sight of him. With as much time as he'd spent out of the office this week dealing with vendor issues, she'd actually missed him.

"You sound surprised." Since she'd already saddled her horse, he cupped his hands to give her a leg up.

"I am." She rested her hands on his shoulders for leverage as she slid onto the back of her horse. This evening, she was riding a gorgeous palomino gelding. His white mane flowed to one side, and his glossy tail draped nearly all the way to the ground. Claire Cassidy had named him Groom, because she insisted he looked like a bridegroom in a beige tuxedo.

Asher saddled a dark brown stallion named Pontius — so dark that part of his coat appeared black — and joined her in the practice ring outside the barn. The stallion's mane and tail were as black as coal. He gave his head an arrogant toss at the sight of Bella riding Groom.

She smiled. "I think Pontius is disappointed I didn't choose to exercise one of his girlfriends this evening." The main reason for the stallion's presence at Cassidy Farm was to breed the mares and produce foals. He also possessed a broody temperament, not unlike his current rider. According to Fox, Asher was the only one the stallion liked very much. Everyone else in the family he treated with disdain, including Fox, who was stuck exercising him most of the time.

"He's a single guy," Asher returned mildly.

"So are you, yet all you've done is complain, complain, complain about that kissing booth."

"First of all, I'm not a horse." Asher spared her a bemused glance as they rode out of the ring and headed toward the nearest wooded trail. "I'm also approaching thirty. Way too old for games like that.

They should've picked a younger guy to fill my spot."

"You're not exactly over the hill yet," she pointed out, "and you're still single." Jade had known exactly what she was doing when she'd strong-armed the Cassidy brothers into the charity event. Their ages ranged from twenty-one to twenty-nine, which gave the hopeful single ladies a whole range of choices.

"Yeah, but you're going to help me convince them otherwise, right?"

"Should I?" Bella nudged her horse into a trot, then waited for him to catch up to her before asking, "Why are you so dead set against dating? And don't tell me it's because of your scars, because I'm not buying it."

He studied her for a moment. "If I give up one of my secrets, you have to give up one of yours."

"Ever the king of evasiveness," she accused.

"Tit for tat, Bella Johnson. That's my final offer."

"If you expect me to give up one of my secrets in return, I want the full truth and nothing but the truth from you."

"So do I."

"Okay. I'm in." She waved at him to continue. "You go first, and I promise to give as good of information as I receive."

He pointed at the distant fence. "Race you to the far end of the pasture first."

Without waiting for her answer, he nudged his stallion into a gallop.

Her heart racing with excitement, Bella urged

Groom to follow him. This was exactly what the horses needed, what they craved. So did she, after a week of being cooped up for hours and hours inside the administrative office. The wide open spaces of Cassidy Farm were both soothing and peaceful. The fresh air, gently waving grasses, and canyon views had a way of restoring one's soul.

When they arrived at the fence, Asher circled Pontius around in a slow trot, then dropped him down to a walk before bringing him to a halt. Hopping to the ground, Asher tethered the beast against the fence and left him to graze. Moving to Bella's side, he reached up to assist her down.

"I'm ready for you this time, Miss Calamity." He made a big show of digging in his heels and bracing himself for her weight.

"Very funny."

"To you, maybe. I'm the one you've bowled over not once, but twice."

"There were extenuating circumstances, and you know it." She rested her hands on his shoulders and allowed him to lift her down.

"You're full of excuses, aren't you? All I know is there's never a dull moment when you're around." He didn't immediately step back or immediately lower his hands from her waist.

"Oh, I beg to differ." She sniffed in disgust as she dropped her hands to her sides. "I've been bored out of my mind dealing with all those address changes. I finally finished them, though." There was nothing fake about the relief in her voice. "I hope to high

Heaven I never see another one of those things as long as I live."

Asher's gaze grew more intent. "Does that mean you're staying in Chipper?"

"Nice try," she stabbed a finger in the direction of his chest, "but I'm not falling for it. You agreed to answer my question first. So shoot. What do you have against dating? For real."

"Nothing."

Disappointment spiraled through her as she tipped her face up to his. "I was expecting more than a one-word answer."

"And I'm about to give you one." He finally stepped away from her, moving to the fence to rest his elbows on it. Gazing out over the distant canyons, he muttered, "I've made too many mistakes. Jade wasn't the only one, though she was, by far, the worst one. As a high school quarterback, I gave in to peer pressure all too often and dated who I was expected to — homecoming queen, cheer captain, you name it."

"And Jade was?" Bella prodded.

"Captain of the cheerleading squad. Beautiful, popular, and fun to be around. We dated off and on through high school and afterward. Everyone expected us to get married...eventually. I was actually close to popping the question right before the fire took place. For months afterward, I actually blamed the fire for ruining that opportunity. How stupid is that?"

Bella moved to stand beside him at the fence.

"What do you think kept you from proposing to her?"

"I've asked myself that a thousand times." He gripped the fence. "I'm not sure. All I can tell you is, Jade and I never had what my parents do, and that's what I want. If I can't have it, I've decided I'd rather stay single."

"So you don't date at all anymore?"

He shrugged. "Not since the fire."

"Because of your scars?"

"At first, yes. But lately, no. I just don't want to make another mistake." He gave Bella a sidelong glance. "If I ever take that plunge again, I want to be her Mr. Right. I'm done being Mr. Not Right. There are too many of those kinds of relationships in the world, and they never last."

"Okay, now I'm confused. How does fake dating me solve anything?" She understood the sentiments behind his words. She certainly knew what it felt like to be wrong for someone and to have one's heart crushed in the process. She also sympathized with his fears about making another mistake. But life was full of risks, wasn't it?

"It doesn't solve anything." He grunted. "At best, it'll buy me a little time. My parents aren't trying too hard to hide the fact that their next big mission in life is getting all six of their sons married off. I'm just not ready for that. After everything that's happened to me, I may never be ready."

The bleakness in his voice tore at her heart. "Fair enough. One last follow up question, then you can tear into my equally sorry story," she promised. "Why fake date me instead of someone else? Is it because I'm new in town?"

"No. It's because you never got hung up on my scars. You've always seen past them. Always treated me like a human being. We have real conversations. And when I push your buttons, you get genuinely mad at me."

Bella stared at him, aghast. "You make it sound like you've been pushing my buttons on purpose!"

He shrugged. "I was trying to find your walk-away point."

Her fingers itched to slap him. "What's a walk-away point?"

He shrugged again. "Every woman has one. You know what I mean. It's when they get everything they want from a guy, then move on."

"Actually, I have no idea what you're talking about." She was furious at his insinuation that all women could be lumped into the same mold. "I've never treated any guy like that." She always gave as much as she took.

"Oh, come on!" He cast another sideways glance at her. "You were talking about leaving from the moment you arrived. All you needed was some money in the bank first."

"That's not the same thing," she protested. "You were talking about messing with a guy's head in a romantic way, and I would never do that. Not intentionally, anyway."

He abruptly changed the subject. "So, what is it

that you really want, Bella Johnson? You say you need money, but I've always suspected it's more than that. I know it's none of my business, but I worry about you sometimes. I worry about when you're going to leave and how I'm ever going to find anyone else to put up with me and my garbage. I worry about you when you get that look on your face that tells me you're only waiting for the other shoe to drop."

"Are you asking as my employer?" she inquired when he fell silent.

"Definitely, but I'm also asking as your friend."

"We're friends?" she teased, trying not to read too much into the warmth his words flooded her with. "Boy, I did *not* get that out of any of our previous conversations."

"Whatever. You're my fake girlfriend, so I obviously don't hate you. Answer the question already." He turned around to rest his forearms against the fence and gazed back toward the ranch.

"I, um…" *Oh, man!* This was so hard to talk about. "I just want the pain to stop, I guess. I want to keep running until it can't catch up with me anymore." Without warning, her eyes flooded with tears.

"Hey, hey, hey!" Asher leaned her way in concern. "I didn't mean to unchain the Kraken here."

"It's okay." She made a face at him through her tears. "I laugh at inappropriate times, and I cry over nothing at other times. You should be used to my insanity by now."

"The pain you mentioned doesn't sound like nothing. Who hurt you?" he demanded in such a fierce tone that she smiled.

"The other boss I dated. He was the high school principal where I worked. It was against the rules for us to date, so we did it in secret. It was exciting at first, really exciting. And fun." More tears rolled down her cheeks. "Until I found out I wasn't the only teacher he was dating."

"What a scumbag!"

"That's not even the worst of it." *In for a penny.* Asher had been brutally honest with her, and she'd promised to do the same. "He proposed right after Gram passed away. She was my last living family, so it hit really hard. I think that's why I was so quick to say yes to marriage, even though we hadn't dated long. I wanted a family so bad. I wanted to belong to someone in this world again." She drew a deep breath. "To matter." Family was like an anchor. Without them, a person felt lost and adrift.

Asher silently reached for her hand. "You matter to me, Bella."

She sniffed damply, appreciating his words but knowing he had no real understanding of what she was talking about. "You've only known me for a couple of weeks."

"So?"

"I'm talking about family, Asher. What you and your parents and brothers have. A lifetime of shared experiences and memories. Can you even imagine what the world would feel like without them in it?"

"No."

"Or how empty your life would be if you'd never had them in it?" She'd never known who her father was, and her mother had died so young.

"I can't imagine such a thing." He laced his fingers through hers. "I wouldn't be who I am today without them. It's more than shared experiences and memories. My life is indelibly intertwined with theirs."

"It is," she agreed brokenly. "Not only wouldn't you be the same person, you would go to bed each night with a nagging feeling that you were missing something. It's an emptiness that no words can adequately describe. A sense that there's something more out there to be had, but it's just out of your reach."

"Come here, Bella." He used their joined hands to tug her closer.

"What are you doing?"

"Hugging you."

"I'm not sure why," she mumbled, though she didn't resist when he enclosed her in his embrace.

"Because I want to."

"That's not much of an answer."

"You don't have to psycho-analyze everything."

She tipped her head against his shoulder, finally giving in to the temptation to just be with him. They were like two ships that had been battered by two different storms, bent but not broken, weary but not sunk.

He smelled of horses, dirt, and sweat. All male.

And for the moment, he was all hers. But not for long. Once their fake dating gig was over, Bella could only presume they would go their separate ways again.

"I can't take away your sadness or your pain," he mused against her hairline. "I wish I could, but I can't. I also can't promise I won't pound the snot out of your ex if he dares to show up here."

She smiled at the anger reverberating in his voice. "Did you ever call the school for a reference check?" She tipped her face up to scan his expression, inadvertently bringing their lips closer together — much closer. She eyed his hard mouth breathlessly, wondering what it would feel like to have it pressed against hers.

"No."

"Good." She quickly dipped her head against his shoulder again. "Then maybe he won't find me for a while this time."

His arms tightened around her. "Has he threatened you?"

"No. He actually keeps insisting he wants to get back together. He claims what happened in Dallas with the other teacher was all just a big misunderstanding."

"Is that what you really want, Bella? Reconciliation with this guy?"

"No way!" She shivered and burrowed closer. "Like you, I just want to be left alone. I keep telling him that."

"Ever thought about getting a restraining order on this joker?"

"Yes, but those things take time and money." Two things she rarely had much of. She gave Asher's midsection one last squeeze before stepping back. "Thanks for the hug."

"Welcome." He dropped his arms. "I have a big family, Bella."

"I am aware." *Way to state the obvious.*

"And we always stick together."

"I bet." Envy shot through her. *Do you really have to keep rubbing it in?*

"As long as you stay here at Cassidy Farm, you can tap into that."

"That's a nice thing to say, but—"

"No buts." He lightly pressed a finger to her lips. "I know they're not yours the way they're mine, but you can still tap into what we have. I'm a farmer, so I know all about transplanting. You can be a part of this company, this community, and this family for as long as you want. Just like plants, people can grow new roots."

Her eyes grew damp again. "That may be the nicest thing anyone has ever said to me."

"Glad I could help." He angled his head at the horses. "You ready to go change into that dress?"

"I am." She took one last look at the canyons before allowing him to swing her back up on the horse.

It was such a beautiful place and such a beautiful moment that she was reluctant to leave it. Something had changed between her and Asher while they were having their heart-to-heart. Maybe it was the way he'd listened, or maybe it was his hug afterward. All she knew was that she felt less alone in the world during their ride back.

CHAPTER 5: EX MARKS THE SPOT

ASHER

MORE THAN A YEAR had passed since Asher's last dinner date. He showered, shaved, and patted on some aftershave, wishing he'd taken the time to head into town earlier for a haircut. Unlike Fox, who liked to wear his dark mane on the longer and shaggier side, Asher had always preferred a sports cut — extra short on the sides with just a tad more on top.

Instead of blue jeans, he pulled on a pair of beige denim ones. In lieu of a plaid shirt, he pulled on a brown henley, snug enough to show he'd been working out. He'd lost way too much weight while he was in the hospital, including muscle. It had taken many slow and painful months in his home gym to recover his full strength. Lots of arm curls and squats, plus hours on the bench press machine — sticking to his workout day after day after day.

When he'd hugged Bella this afternoon, he hoped she was at least a little impressed by the progress he'd made. He wasn't sure why it mattered since they weren't really dating, but it did. He liked her more than he should and hoped they would have the chance to get to know each other better before she took off again. That was the kicker. She wasn't in Chipper to stay. For this reason, he needed to keep his emotional distance from her — to be friends and enjoy being with her while he could, but not get too attached. Though he was over Jade, he wasn't ready to have his heart broken again. He might never be ready.

It was the one thing he'd kept from Bella during their soul-bearing fest today — his fear that he'd already used up whatever it was that allowed a man to love a woman. Maybe his last chance at that kind of happiness had already passed. Maybe the fire had burned it right out of him.

Before he left the bathroom, he turned his face to allow the damaged side of it to fill the mirror over the sink, trying to see what Bella saw when she looked at him. The same scarred man that stared back at him every morning was still there, leaving him no closer to an answer.

Huffing out a resigned breath, he returned to the master bedroom to lift his Stetson from the bedpost. He pressed it to his head as he headed out the door. Bella still didn't know about the home he'd custom built, and he had no plans to tell her yet. He wasn't ready to share his private oasis from the rest of the world with her or anyone else. Though he'd once pictured Jade living here with him, he'd not brought her by for a single visit before they broke up. In hindsight, he was glad there were no memories of her between these four walls, no sadness to encroach on the sacredness of the place.

When he'd reached the age of twenty-five, his parents had deeded off twenty acres of prime land with canyon views to him. They'd done the same for each of his brothers on their twenty-fifth birthdays. He and Beldon had both chosen to build homes in the center of theirs.

Beldon was the lead herdsman and range rider for Cassidy Farm, and he was just as committed as Asher about remaining in the family business. Cormac was a farmer at heart, like their dad, and spent most of his time out in the fields. He was currently trading house plans back and forth with an architect and hoped to start building by mid-summer. Devlin and Emerson had only recently turned twenty-five. Neither of them had yet decided what they were going to do with their land. They were budding businessmen who did the lion's share of work required to run the store and coffee shop. They were content to continue sharing the hunting cabin on the main property that Mom had recently upgraded with all modern appliances and amenities. Like their three older brothers, however, they were equally committed to Cassidy Farm.

At the age of twenty-three, Fox was the only brother who'd not yet been gifted any land. So far, he also hadn't given his family any indication of his plans for the future. He'd opted not to attend college in lieu of competing on the rodeo circuit. It was a dangerous and volatile career that kept him out of town for months on end. Their mother made no attempt to hide her many hopes and prayers that he would return home some day. For good.

Asher paused at the cathedral window in his two-story living room. He'd deliberately built this room to face the canyons. On clear days, they stretched in craggy pinks and blues as far as the eye could see. On dusty days, they rose like hazy giants in the distance. As sure as he was standing there, he would never get tired of looking at them.

That was the other reason he put the brakes on his dating life. The day he'd moved into his new home, he'd put down some pretty permanent roots in Texas. He was in Chipper to stay. And until he found a woman who wanted to put down roots beside him and share this view for the rest of their lives, well... like he'd told Bella earlier, he'd reached the point where he'd just rather do without.

She hadn't said much about his offer to share his farm, family, and community. It was almost like she didn't really believe him.

She'd wanted to. He could sense that. It wasn't something he could ever force, though. Like every other person in the world, Bella was going to have to find her own way. No one could do it for her. She was going to have to take life by the horns and fight for what she wanted. In the end, only she could decide where and when she would put down roots. All he could do was show her the possibilities of doing it in his town.

He exited the living room of his two-story log home, hoping she would ultimately do what he had — choose to stay. It was an easier decision for him, because he'd been born and raised in this town. He had family here. He belonged. All Bella was and ever would be was a transplant. But so were a lot of the crops on Cassidy Farm. Years ago, his grandfather had imported the finest seeds and seedlings from all over the world. He'd experimented with hybrids in greenhouses until he'd come up with the exact results he'd wanted. And now even the transplants looked, felt, and tasted liked they belonged.

Asher's parents had spent their entire adult lives growing his legacy, cultivating his precious plants and tending and expanding his precious herds. They expected their sons to do the same.

But for tonight, Asher was taking a break from it — from his family's legacy and all the expectations and pressures that accompanied it. He was going to escort Bella to dinner, try to remember what it felt like to be twenty-nine, and simply enjoy being in the presence of such a lovely date.

Asher usually drove a classic white Chevy when it came to work around the farm. Tonight, however, he decided to drive his pickup, a sleek black Ram with a dual cab. It was less than six months old and still had that new car smell clinging to its leather seats.

"Date night," he muttered beneath his breath as he started the ignition and rolled it from his garage. It took less than five minutes to traverse the gravel road leading back to the main part of Cassidy Farm. The sun was setting on the fences, pastures, and metal barn roofs.

As he pulled up to the front of the entrance of the horse barn, one of the side doors opened and Bella stepped out.

Asher stared for a moment, speechless, as she sauntered his way in a white sundress with spaghetti straps. Gone was the ranch hand in braids that he'd hired two weeks ago. She still had on her Stetson and boots, but they were new — both of them. And her hair. *Wow!*

He whistled beneath his breath at the sight of her long, chestnut tresses waving in the breeze against her arms and shoulders. She was stunning, right down to the sprinkling of freckles across her nose and cheek bones.

He finally jolted into action, throwing open the driver's door and hurrying around to swing open the passenger door for her. "You look good." More than good. He drank in the sight of her, knowing he was staring.

A wrinkle formed in the middle of her forehead. "Are you feeling alright?"

"Yeah. Why?"

"You look funny." She scanned his expression anxiously — not his scars, but his eyes. That was just the way she was, always going for the money shot, always caring for the man inside. "You sure everything's okay?"

"This is my stunned look, Bella."

"Oh." A chuckle escaped her. "Is this the part where we hug again?"

"If you want." He certainly wouldn't complain about having her back in his arms.

"Okay. My turn this time." There was a soft look he'd not seen in her dark eyes before as she stretched on her tiptoes to wrap her slender arms around his neck.

He hugged her back, adoring her lithe cowgirl strength and the soapy scent of her. He couldn't detect any perfume or makeup, neither of which surprised him. It wasn't as if her sun-kissed features needed it. *Shoot!* If he wanted to see any more color in her face, he'd already learned more than a dozen ways to make her blush with everything from mortification to anger to pleasure.

Of all his options, though, he preferred it when she was happy.

A frenzy of barking broke out in the distance. It was followed by a crunch of gravel as it grew nearer.

Asher scowled over the top of Bella's head at the white German Shepherd barreling their way. "Don't even think about it," he snarled, lifting a warning finger. There was an extra spring in the dog's step as he bounded in their direction, tongue lolling in excitement.

"Ghost!" Fox hollered, sprinting after him.

"What's going on?" Mystified, Bella twirled around in Asher's arms, her hands sliding down to his biceps in the process. He gave them a quick flex for her benefit, though he wasn't sure she noticed. "Ah. We have company."

At the last second, Asher shoved Bella behind him and braced himself for the pouncing he was about to receive. It didn't come.

Ghost skidded to a halt when he reached the toe of his boots.

"Good boy!" Bella praised in her musical voice. "Good boy! Very good boy. I'll have to bring you some special treats in the morning."

The dog gave a yodel of excitement, as if he'd understood every word she said, and broke into a prance of celebration. However, he still didn't jump on them. For all intents and purposes, he ran in place, but that was it.

"What did you do to the guy?" Asher reached behind him for Bella's hand. "Cast a spell on him?"

She placed her hand in his. "Nothing that exciting. I've just been working with him a little."

"Uh-huh," he returned dryly. "From my angle, it looks like I'm dating a dog whisperer."

She leaned against his shoulder. "Fake dating," she reminded softly.

Right. It no longer felt fake to him, though. From the way Fox was eyeing them, Asher could only imagine the questions springing up in his youngest brother's mind about what was going on between him and Bella. *Bug off, bro! Not your business.* He shot him a warning glare.

Fox merely grinned and whistled for his dog.

After a longing yip in Bella's direction, Ghost obediently trotted back to his owner.

Asher and Bella were soon cruising along the two-lane highway toward the main part of town. "I probably should've offered to drive you to Amarillo. There are a lot more restaurants to choose from there."

"It would've taken longer," she pointed out reasonably, "and our target audience is here in Chipper."

He raised his eyebrows at her. "Target audience?" He pretended confusion. "Is that school teacher jargon?"

"More like basic business jargon," she returned in a scoffing voice. "You should already be well versed in it, Mr. Ranch Manager."

"Nah, it's your job to cross my T's and keep my commas in the right place," he drawled.

"Here and I thought my job was to do whatever you woke up and decided to assign me each morning."

"That, too." He shot her a curious look. "Do you think I'm too hard on you?" The day he'd hired her, all he'd wanted was someone to pick up the slack on the grunt work around the farm. However, from the start, he'd discovered her good opinion mattered to him. So, any time he gave her something difficult to do, he made sure he had his own sleeves rolled up, working alongside her. They were a pretty incredible team. She saw things he didn't and often gave him a different perspective. She both entertained him and kept him sharp. He was starting to dread the day he would have to carry on without her.

She was silent as they drove up to the crowded diner. Glancing over at him, she seemed to be trying to choose her words carefully. "You're tough, but fair. I don't have any complaints."

Asher's shoulders relaxed as he circled around the parking lot twice to find a spot. "If you had any complaints, would you tell me?"

"Would you want me to?" she countered.

"Very much, so spill if you've got any."

"I don't."

"Not a single one?" He was incredulous as he pushed open his door.

"You'll be the first to know if that changes." She opened the passenger door before he could reach her. However, she waited for him to assist her to the pavement.

"Show time!" he muttered in her ear.

She gave a slight shiver.

"Cold?" he asked quickly.

"No, I, ah…" Her voice sounded strained, then she lapsed into silence.

"What's wrong?" He slid an arm around her shoulders and tugged her closer.

"Who said anything's wrong?" she muttered, but she melted bonelessly against him.

Feeling her tremble, he retorted, "I do."

"It's that Porsche over there." She pointed weakly in the direction of the silver bullet of a sports car.

Yeah, he agreed it looked out of place. "You don't like Porsches?"

"Not anymore." She shivered again. "Especially ones with Dallas plates on them."

Then he understood. "You trying to tell me that's what your ex drove?"

Instead of answering, she nodded against his shoulder. "Want to just turn around and go back home?" she asked breathlessly. "Please?"

Home. Even as apprehension spread like acid across his tongue, he liked the way the word slid so easily from her lips. Cassidy Farm had built their brand on family values. It made him feel good that Bella was buying into the magic of the place. And no way was he letting her give up on it this soon.

"We could, darling, if that's what you really want." Not caring that they were in a public place, he paused just outside the chrome and glass door to tip her chin up. "Or we can stay and face your demons together. If that's really him inside, he'll have to go through me to get to you. You have my word." Better yet. He reached for his cell phone and pulled up the SOS thread he and his brothers had started a few years back. *Diner,* he typed. *ASAP.*

Bella watched him type. "What are you doing?" she asked nervously.

"Calling in reinforcements. My brothers will be here in two snaps. Count on it." He held her gaze as he pocketed his phone again. "So, what's it going to be? Hold our ground or run? Your call."

She anxiously scanned his features. "The bald

truth is, I'm tired, Asher. Tired of being afraid. Tired of running."

"That's my girl." He wanted to kiss her. Badly. However, this wasn't the time.

"You're doing it again," she whispered.

"Doing what?"

"Looking at me that way."

"It's not my fault you're beautiful."

"Asher!" she gasped, chuckling.

"What?"

"I can't always tell when you're being serious as opposed to when you're playing a role. It all sort of runs together."

"Does it matter?" It was all running together for him, too. He'd discovered it wasn't necessary to play a role when he was with her. Acting like he cared for her came all too naturally.

She gave another nervous-sounding chuckle. "Not as long as you help me sort it all out later — what's real and what's not."

He pulled open the door of the diner and stepped inside, keeping her anchored against his side. The moment they joined the long line snaking its way to the check-in booth, he dipped his head over hers. "I'm gonna make fake googly eyes at my fake girlfriend, but I'm going to give her a real kiss," he finished in a rough voice as he brushed his lips against hers.

Her warm lips moved beneath his. "Real kiss?" she squeaked.

"Yeah. Because I forgot to research how to give a

girl a fake kiss," he joked. "Are fake kisses even a thing?"

"No idea. This is unchartered territory for me, too." Her voice was tremulous against his mouth as his lips found hers again.

Yes, darlin'. Just like this. He felt like he'd waited an eternity to sample her sweetness. She tasted like sunshine and hope, with a side of cautious joy.

At some point during their kiss, she ever-so-softly palmed his scarred cheek. That was the moment he realized there'd be no coming back from their kiss — not that he had any desire to.

The line in front of them moved all too quickly. When they reached the hostess station, it took an extra effort to keep his voice even. "Table for seven," he requested. He was breathing like a guy who'd just finished running a half marathon.

"This is a diner." The young woman in a striped apron rolled her eyes at him. "You can have two booths, two tables, or a booth and a table when they clear that spot over there." She nodded across the room where a bus boy was busy wiping down a table.

"We'll take two booths, please."

"Certainly, sir. If you'll just follow me."

As she led them across the crowded dining room, a man exclaimed, "Bella? Bella Johnson?" There was a frantic tenor to his voice. "Is it really you?"

"As if he didn't already know," Bella's fingernails dug into Asher's hand, "considering how he stalked me all the way from Dallas."

"Play it cool," Asher muttered in her ear, "and act bored. Make him feel like last year's news."

"Right." She gave a shaky chuckle and straightened her shoulders as she gazed around them. Though her hand still clung to his, she managed to feign surprise at the man in a gray pinstriped suit making a beeline for her. "Hey, Jake!"

The man scowled in consternation at her. "Who's Jake? It's me, Jim."

Clever, darlin'. Trying not to laugh at the realization that Bella had purposefully misstated the man's name, Asher stared sourly at his pinky ring and designer dress shoes. *Dude, this is the backwoods of Texas.* The guy's suit stuck out like an ultra lame attempt at making a fashion statement. *Wrong town. Wrong restaurant.* As the man's dark, beady gaze roved hungrily over Bella, Asher tightened his arm around her shoulders and mentally added, *wrong woman.*

"Oh, right. Jim." She smiled up at Asher. "This is my boyfriend, Asher."

He ignored her introduction, along with the man standing next to her. "We need to talk," he said brusquely.

"About?" To Asher's amazement, she actually managed to fake a yawn. "Oh, gosh! Sorry about that. It's been a long week, hasn't it, babe?" She glanced up at him again as if expecting some sort of confirmation.

"I survived," he announced in a teasing voice, "but only because of you." He swooped in for another floor-shaking kiss. It was the only way to describe it, because he was pretty sure he felt the floor shake beneath his boots. *Good gravy!* Fake relationship or not, he decided on the spot that he was never going to get tired of kissing this particular woman. It was a problem he hadn't seen coming. Lord willing, it wouldn't be an insurmountable one.

"If you don't mind," the man declared testily, "I'd like to speak to Bella. Alone. We have some unresolved—"

"I mind." Asher abruptly raised his head. "In case you didn't notice, I'm on a dinner date with my girl, and I'm not all that interested in acquiring a third wheel." Out of the corner of his eye, he watched the diner door open. Five broad-shouldered men with familiar faces filed in. *Right on time.*

"Listen, if you'd rather take this outside." Her ex's voice took on a nasty edge.

"Don't mind if we do." Beldon's quiet voice broke through the general hum and babble of restaurant noise.

Asher glanced over to meet his brother's gaze, giving him a nearly imperceptible nod of thanks.

His five brothers closed in, forming a loose semi-circle behind Bella's ex-fiancé.

Jim spun around to face the newest arrivals. "Bug off, buddy! This is a private conversation."

When Beldon didn't budge, he demanded, "Who in the heck are you, anyway?"

"Family," Beldon returned in a voice as smooth as

icicles. "We're with them." He tipped his head toward Asher and Bella.

Jim visibly deflated as he eyed the cluster of brothers. All five of them had their arms crossed in a way that made their chests and biceps bulge. "So, ah, I'm not looking for any trouble."

"Good to hear," Cormac returned easily, leaning closer. His movement further crowded Jim's space, making him take another half-step back. "Anything we can help you with?"

"As a matter of fact, I have some unfinished business with Bella Johnson, and this guy isn't—"

"Consider it finished," Beldon's voice turned steely.

"If you'll just hear me out." Fury flamed across Jim's wide face as he turned to face Beldon, hands balled on his hips. "A little over a year ago, Bella and I became engaged—"

"And now you're not."

"I still have a right to have a conversation with her."

"Only if she agrees to it." Beldon's face grew as hard as flint. "You see, here in Chipper, Texas, women have rights, too."

"You know what? You're impossible!" Throwing up his hands, Jim whirled around to face Asher and Bella again. "Bella, just tell these-these *cowboys* we need to talk." It was clear he'd wanted to use a stronger word to describe his listeners, but he had the sense to tone it down a bit.

"About?" There was a faint tremor in Bella's voice

that made Asher furious all over again. He hovered protectively at her side, silently encouraging her to hang in there a little longer. At the same time, he shot a warning look at his brothers, knowing they needed to put an end to the confrontation before things got out of hand.

"Us! I want to talk about us!" Jim's voice rose several decibels, causing heads to turn in their direction.

"Well, I don't wish to have that conversation," she returned firmly. "It's over, Jim. You know that. It's been over." Though she looked and sounded strained, her choice of words left no room for quibbling.

"But you've never let me explain! I know you don't love me anymore, but I still love you, and I want to make things right." He waved his hands angrily at her. "That's why I've been trying—"

"You heard the lady," Fox interrupted, stepping up to one side of the man while Beldon closed in on his other side. Asher had never heard his youngest brother use that exact tone of voice before. It held a note of bleak finality, making him sound much older than his twenty-three years. "This is the part where you walk away."

With a muttered expletive, Jim swung away from Bella at last, and tried to plow his way through the Cassidy brothers. They didn't move, so he didn't get very far.

"By walk away, I meant walk around." Fox made no attempt to hide his sarcasm.

"This isn't over," Jim seethed through gritted teeth. Asher doubted it was possible for the man's face to turn any redder without exploding a blood vessel.

"Actually, it is, because she said it was." Fox's expression was formidable. "You give her any more trouble, and you'll be dealing with the law."

"Whatever," the man growled.

"Oh, my lands!" Bella whispered as he finally stormed from the diner. She wilted against Asher, who hastily ushered her inside the booth.

The diner hostess was staring at them with her red-painted mouth agape. She finally closed it and leaned over the table to set a pair of menus in front of them. "For a sec there, I thought I might have to call 911 or something."

"Two teas, please. Unsweet with plenty of lemon," Asher said quietly, anxious to be alone with Bella again.

"Ah, okay. I'll let your waitress know." With one last uncertain look at them, she walked away muttering something about how she couldn't wait for her shift to be over.

Beldon and Cormac slid into the booth across from them, while their other three brothers took a seat in the empty booth adjacent to them.

"Hey." Beldon met Asher's gaze. "Is she okay?"

"I'm fine," Bella assured in a thready voice. "Really." But she continued to grip Asher's hand like a lifeline beneath the table.

Beldon nodded. "Looks like the coast is clear, so

we're gonna dash. Fox has some errands to run, so he won't be too far away for the next hour. The rest of us will stay glued to our phones."

"Thanks." Asher balled a hand, and they exchanged a round of fist bumps.

Beldon nodded. "That's what family's for." He motioned for Cormac to scoot out of the booth ahead of him.

As his brothers strode from the diner, Asher stretched out his legs in front of him, getting comfortable. Giving Bella's hand a gentle squeeze, he spoke without looking at her. "Call me crazy, but it's starting to feel like there's more to what's going on with your ex than what you've told me so far."

Bella started to pull her hand away from his.

"I thought you said you were ready to quit running." He turned his head and met her troubled gaze. "Whatever you're afraid of, I'm right here. You're not alone anymore."

She caught her lower lip between her teeth. "Dragging you into my problems was never part of the deal."

"Really? Because I didn't think twice about dragging you into mine," he informed her bluntly.

She briefly closed her eyes. "I know you mean well, Asher, but please don't try to twist my words. I don't want to bleed my problems all over you and your wonderful family. Please try to respect that."

"Look at me, Bella." He waited until she opened her eyes again. "What do you see?"

To his consternation, her eyes grew damp. "One

of the nicest people I've ever met, despite your asinine amount of grumbling, grumping, and growling."

He grinned at her. "Thanks, I think, but that's not what I was getting at. My point is, my life hasn't been a bed of roses, either. The difference between you and me is, I've had family to lean on, whereas you had no one." He paused to let that sink in. "Until now."

"Please don't do this." As she shook her head at him, a fresh round of tears festered and gathered in her eyes. "I'm not bringing my mess one step further into your life or your brothers' lives. I just…can't."

His heart sang at what she left unsaid. "Because you care about us, huh?"

"Of course I do!" She cried in a low, strangled voice. "That's why this is so hard. I know what I need to do. I just don't want to."

"Then don't." He instinctively knew she was referring to running again. "Don't leave Cassidy Farm, Bella. Don't leave me."

"Why? You're not even my real boyfriend!" she protested.

"I could be."

"I don't want your pity." She glanced away from him, blinking hard.

"I think we both know I didn't kiss you out of pity, darlin'." He'd wanted to kiss her. Badly. And he was ready to do it again.

"We shouldn't have done that." She gave a loud sniffle. "I should have never suggested this whole fake relationship thing. I shouldn't have—"

"Too late," he informed her quietly. "We did, you did, and there's no putting that cat back in the bag. Quite frankly, I don't want to."

Her head whipped back to him so quickly that her hair brushed his arm. "What are you saying?"

"Let me in, Bella." He gestured between them. "Be my girlfriend. For real this time."

She paled a little. "I don't know what to say."

It wasn't a hard no. Her hesitation gave him the courage to try a different tactic. "If our circumstances were different…if they were better, would you date a guy like me?"

She blinked. "You know I would."

"Then let's do it."

"Asher," she sighed.

"I get it. Life has given us both a few lemons." He reached over to tuck a stray strand of hair behind her ear. "So let's make some lemonade together."

For a moment, hope warred with the despair swimming in her lustrous dark eyes.

"Oh, for Pete's sake, Bella!" he exploded. "Just say yes. You know you want to."

CHAPTER 6: MUSIC TO THEIR EARS

BELLA

BELLA'S LIPS parted in amazement as she read the silent pleading in Asher's gaze. They were as blue as the Texas sky outside and filled with adoring determination. "Why me?" Confusion swept through her. She'd asked before, but she really wanted to know.

"Listen, I'm not ever gonna have the smooth and polished answers you deserve. You should know that by now. I can't even sit here and claim, beyond a shadow of doubt, that I'm the right guy for you." His jaw tightened. "All I know is, I want to be."

Uncertainty swam through her, grappling with the glimmer of hope he was offering her. "If you knew the extent of my problems, you might change your tune." There. She'd finally put the worst of her fears into words.

"I doubt it." The grim certainty in his voice was reassuring.

"The rest of my story isn't a pretty one."

"Talk to me, Bella."

Their waitress arrived with their drinks. "Hey, y'all. I'm Tink as in Tinkerbell. What sounds good to you this evening?" She tossed her ponytail over her shoulder as she set their iced tea glasses on the table. "Burgers? Chicken-fried steak? I promise our food will make your evening better."

"It's already the best night of my life." Asher reached over to lightly touch Bella's cheek. "I just need to do a little better job at convincing this gal." He dropped his hand. "Do you need more time to look at the menu, darlin'?"

"No, I'm ready." Bella forced a smile she didn't feel as apprehension curdled through her. "I'd like a wedge salad, please. No croutons."

Tink nodded, scrawling a note on her order pad. "We normally drizzle it with our hand-mixed blue cheese dressing and world-famous vinaigrette."

"Sounds amazing."

"And you?" The waitress glanced over at Asher.

"One of those double cheeseburgers for me, extra bonfire sauce and a double order of fries." He winked at Bella. "In case you change your mind."

She didn't miss the double entendre behind his words. As their waitress walked away, she made a face at him. "I see what you did there."

"Don't try to change the subject."

She tipped her head back to stare at the ceiling. "God, give me strength," she whispered. Then she met Asher's gaze. "After Jim and I got engaged, I cashed out my life savings and retirement plan with the school district so we could buy a house together. Since his apartment lease was up for renewal, he moved in right away to save money. The plan was for me to ride out the rest of my apartment lease and join him there after we got married. Unfortunately, I found out he was cheating on me with a fellow school teacher before that happened." She waved a nerveless hand. "I begged him to either sell the house or give me back my money. He refused."

Asher leaned back against the seat cushion, scowling into the distance.

"Say something," she pleaded.

"Relax. I still want to date you."

"Okay." She felt her cheeks turn pink.

"Okay? That's all you've got to say after everything we've been through together?" He turned his head suddenly to capture her mouth with his.

She giggled and kissed him back. Happiness welled inside her, along with the relief of knowing that he hadn't tucked tail and run from the ugliness she was up to her neck in. She was well aware it was going to require an attorney to help her sort through it, but it wasn't something she could afford right now.

"And now you're laughing at me," he growled against her lips.

"No. Only at myself," she confessed ruefully. "I honestly can't believe you're still sitting next to this hot mess."

"Really? Then let me spell it out for you." His hooded gaze clashed with hers, sending a thousand beams of warmth and wonder through her. "I like you, Bella. A lot."

"I like you, too. Sometimes," she added in a teasing voice.

He leaned in to brush his mouth against hers again. "Guess I'll have to work on that." He didn't look too worried about it, though, as he drew back to study her. "So, you own a house."

"Co-own," her lips twisted wryly, "though his contribution was a lot bigger than mine."

"Did you both sign the paperwork?"

"Yes."

"Was there a prenup?"

"No." Jim had been very much in favor of signing a prenuptial agreement, probably due to her much humbler finances, but something had fallen through with it before it happened.

"Then the amount of your contribution doesn't matter. You own it fifty-fifty." He wagged a finger at her. "That's how home deeds work."

"That's my understanding, which is why I begged him to just return my part of the investment. Told him we'd both walk away with what we started off with, the same as if we'd had a prenup in place. However, he swore up and down that I needed to sign over the house to him first. I said no way, because I'd sunk every penny I owned into it and didn't trust him to keep his word. By then, his word wasn't worth spit. Long story short, we never came to an agreement about the money, and he has yet to return a penny of it. When he made noises about not being able to work with me anymore because of it, I figured he was aiming to get me fired from the school district. I sort of lost it and left town. My Gram had just passed, and I was already in a bad place." She grimaced. "Every few months, he tracks me down and hounds me some more about making things right between us. A few months ago, he actually went down on one knee and begged me all over again to marry him. As if that would magically solve anything at this point!"

"It wouldn't." Asher snorted. "What you need is a good attorney to force that joker's hand. Doesn't sound like he plans to do the right thing by you without a little legal nudging."

"I tried," she grimaced, "but that requires funds I don't have."

"Then I'll give you an advance on your pay."

"Asher, no." She shook her head fiercely. "I meant what I said about not pulling you into my garbage. I'll get it sorted out. Eventually."

He studied her for a moment, toying with her fingers. "Would you at least be willing to meet with our family attorney? If you told him what's going on, I'm betting he'd do the work first and let you pay him after you get what's coming to you."

She shrugged. "You think I haven't asked that question before? Believe me, I have, and every attorney I've met with said that's not how it works. None of them would move forward with my case before I produced their up-front retainer fees."

"Of course, they prefer to get paid first. Who

wouldn't? But there's no law that says they have to."
He nodded across the restaurant at someone he must
know. Though he wasn't smiling, there was a light in
his eyes she hadn't seen before. "Our attorney would
take your case." He returned his full attention to her.
"I'm willing to bet my boots on it."

"Now that's saying something!" She pretended
amazement. "We all know how much you love your
boots."

He still didn't crack a smile. "Then you know
how serious I am."

She did. "Gosh, Asher!" She grew serious. "If
you're right about this, I'd be more than happy to
meet with the guy."

"I'm right about a lot of things, Bella Johnson."
He lifted her hand to his lips, his gaze twinkling
knowingly as he brushed his warm mouth across her
fingers.

"Cocky!" She made a face at him.

He gave her a slow wink. "But not wrong."

Their food arrived while she was sticking her
tongue out at him.

"Wow!" Her wedge salad was far bigger than
she'd been expecting, and it was drizzled with all of
her favorite dressings and toppings. "A few minutes
ago I had zero appetite, and now I'm famished." She
lifted her fork and waved it at him. "Entirely your
fault. It takes a massive amount of body fuel to
handle all the work you throw my way each day."

He reached for her hand and said a quick word of

grace over their food before answering. "What else would you do with your time?"

"Sing." She didn't have to stop and think about it. "Play the guitar. Read a book. Should I keep going, slave driver?"

"Nah, I get the picture." He studied her curiously. "Now that you mention it, I've never gotten to hear you sing or play your guitar before."

She popped the first bite of salad in her mouth, chewed, and swallowed. "I haven't sung a note since I arrived in Chipper. Again, your fault." It had been an exhausting two weeks helping Asher get caught up on all the outstanding paperwork in his office. He'd been so far behind, she wasn't sure how he'd made it without losing a vendor contract or missing a bill payment deadline. However, he was one of those nauseatingly disorganized people who had the uncanny ability of knowing where everything was in his piles. He could literally reach into a stack and pull out the exact piece of paper he needed exactly when he needed it.

"We need to remedy that. Tonight." Asher's voice was matter-of-fact.

She chuckled. "I have to be in the mood to sing."

"Then get in the mood." He took a massive bite of his double burger and lapsed into silence for the next few minutes.

———

When they returned to Cassidy Farm, Asher parked in front of the horse barn but kept the motor idling. "If you run grab your guitar, I promise to drive you somewhere that'll put you in the mood to sing."

"I'll admit it." She wrinkled her nose at him. "You have me intrigued."

"Then hurry back." He made a rat-a-tat sound on the steering wheel with his fists before opening his door and hopping down.

She'd ridden back to the farm in the middle of his truck seat, so she merely scooted closer to the driver's door to hop down. "Aren't you going to give me a hint about where we're going?"

"I'll be right here, Bella Johnson." He gazed deeply into her eyes before letting her shoulders go. "Waiting for you."

Taking that as a no, she rolled her eyes and moved around him. Jogging up the stairs two at a time, she retrieved her guitar case and jogged back down the stairs just as quickly.

A man-sized shadow at the bottom of the stairs made her jolt and squeal.

It was Fox. "Oh, my lands, Fox!" She pressed a hand to her heart. "You just shaved a few months off my life."

"Don't worry, beautiful. We have excellent security around here. Mr. Negatron won't be able to waltz in here and scare the bejeebers out of you like I just did."

"Negatron?" She raised her eyebrows questioningly at him. "What's a negatron?" It sounded like something he'd made up.

"According to my nerdy twin brothers, it's science, baby." He gave her a superior smile as he stared down his nose at her. "Inside of every atom are mostly protons, neutrons, and electrons. But occasionally, the universe spits out a mouthful of negative energy like that chucklehead we ran into at the diner."

Aha! She nodded in understanding. "And a negatron is born. Pretty nasty business." It was hilarious that the Cassidys had made up a new word for negative people. It was certainly a fitting description for Jim Steering. He sure had come across as a great guy early on in their relationship, but there had been some clear bursts of negative energy throughout the rest of it. Countless red flags she shouldn't have ignored.

"You okay?" Fox stepped closer to peer down at her in the dim lantern light.

"I am now, thanks to you and your brothers." She gave him a grateful smile. "I don't know how I can ever thank you all."

"Just make Asher happy. That's all the thanks we need."

Her insides gave a nervous flip-flop. "I'll do my best, Fox. That's all I can promise you tonight. In case you haven't noticed, I'm barely keeping it together."

"That's good enough for me." He lightly tapped her shoulder with his fist. "You need anything else, I'm here for you, Bella. We all are."

Unable to think of an appropriate response, she stepped closer to slide an arm around his middle. "Thanks," she whispered.

The honk of a horn outside made her chuckle and step back. "That would be our hard-nosed ranch manager. I'd better get going." She backed toward the door.

"What are you two up to this time?" Fox eyed her guitar case with interest.

"Believe it or not, I think he's expecting a private concert." She rolled her eyes, thankful that the shadows in the barn hid her blushes.

Fox gave a long, low whistle. "Lucky dog!"

Bella hurried outside into the dusky evening.

Asher met her halfway across the gravel driveway on her way to the truck. "What took you so long?" he groused.

"Fox." She laughed.

"Say no more." He swiftly loaded her guitar case into the rear cab and lifted her into the front seat. Then he slid in beside her. "You're going to like where I'm taking you. I guarantee it." He circled around in a small spray of gravel, and they were off again.

Instead of heading back to the main road, he turned off on a narrow gravel driveway that ran between two long pastures.

"This is all part of Cassidy Farm, isn't it?" She stared out the window at the long wooden fence line. Beyond it, hay and alfalfa waved in the evening breeze.

"Yep. My part."

"Your part?" She swiveled in the seat to study his profile. Since it didn't appear that he was staying in the main ranch house with his parents, she'd been wondering where he lived. It looked like she was about to find out.

"Yeah. My parents have this thing they do. Every time one of us turns twenty-five, they deed off some acreage to us. It's their way of solidifying our place in the family business, I think."

"What an incredible legacy!" she breathed, unable to imagine being a part of something so grand. So permanent. She honestly couldn't imagine anything more wonderful than having a family like his.

"Agreed, though I used to be too young and dumb to see it. Like every other snot-nosed kid, I took it for granted while growing up. After the fire, though, I quickly came to the realization that what we have here at Cassidy Farm is special. It's something I hope to be a part of for many years to come."

Laugher bubbled up in Bella's throat.

"What's so funny?" Asher shot her an amused glance.

"It just hit me. That must be why your parents are so anxious to get the matchmaking ball rolling. To keep this legacy going, they're going to need some baby grands running around soon."

"And you find that funny?"

"Oh, yeah. With the way you love to boss people around, the very thought of you having a few of your own whippersnappers…" She stopped and dissolved into snickers.

"Glad someone finds my current crisis so blasted amusing." He drove around a copse of trees on an uphill driveway. Then they were there.

Bella gaped at the two-story cabin rising in front of them. The logs were stained a dark hue of cherry wood. A sunset of rose and purple hues was fingering its way across the sky above it, accentuating each angle and outset of the roofline.

"This is yours?" She blinked and stared some more. The view alone was priceless, better than a painting.

"It's better from the back. Here," Asher urged, reaching behind the seat to retrieve her guitar. "Let's go catch the sunset from the back porch."

Feeling a little dazed, Bella followed wordlessly at his side as they traversed his grassy side yard to mount the steps of his rear veranda. She caught her breath at the realization that it ran the entire length of the house. *Wowsers!* A porch swing was hanging on one side, and a row of rockers were scattered across the rest of it.

"This is incredible." She trailed her fingers over the wooden porch railing, admiring its iron slats and trying to soak it all in. There were evergreens dotting the side yards beyond both ends of the porch, and an owl hooted somewhere in the distance.

Asher deposited her guitar case on the wooden floor planks beside the porch swing. Then he joined her at the railing. "If incredible is what you're looking for," he stretched out one long arm to point at the distant canyons, "keep watching."

So she did, catching her breath in amazement as the skies slowly changed colors. The pinks deepened to purples, turning the canyons below into glowing peaks and craggy drop-offs. Then the purples faded to darker shades of blue, leaving nothing more than the silhouette of the canyons. The moon's rays grew more brilliant as the sun continued to fade. Soon streaks of silver pierced the vast sea of blue. A haze of stars appeared and grew more pronounced. They studded the heavens like diamonds, twinkling whitely.

"How do you ever leave this place?" Bella's voice was hushed with awe. "Even to go to work?"

"Just so I can come back here and watch it all over again." He leaned his forearms on the railing and tipped his head back to gaze upward. "Sometimes I wake up early to come watch those same stars fade back into the sunrise."

There was a reverence in his voice she hadn't heard before. "Have you read that scripture in the Bible about the stars singing?" she inquired softly.

"Yeah. It's in the book of Job." He quoted the first part of it aloud to her. "When the morning stars sang together."

She finished the second half of it for him. "And all the sons of God shouted for joy."

He turned his head to meet her gaze in the moonlight. "My parents said you were at church last Sunday."

She nodded shyly. "I go every chance I get." She'd been disappointed not to see him there with his brothers. Though it was a newer building, it had been constructed in the old, traditional style with a cathedral ceiling, stained glass windows, and a steeple with a church bell.

"I used to." He glanced away from her. "Lately, though, I feel closer to God when I'm out here with the stars."

"They miss you," Bella said softly. "There was an empty place in the pew between your mom and Beldon." She suspected it was where Asher had once stood, since the rest of his brothers stretched shoulder-to-shoulder across the pew in age order — oldest to youngest. Even Fox was there.

"You're kidding."

"I'm not. While the choir was singing, she glanced a few times at the empty place beside her. This is the song they sang." Without any further ado, Bella sang the first few lines of her favorite old hymn.

> "Oh Lord, my God
> When I, in awesome wonder
> Consider all the worlds Thy hands have
>   made.
> I see the stars."

She glanced up at the sky as she continued to sing.

> "I hear the rolling thunder,

*Thy power throughout the universe
    displayed."*

To her surprise, Asher joined his baritone voice
with her soprano one when she reached the chorus.

*"Then sings my soul, my Savior God to
    Thee,
How great Thou art, how great Thou art.
Then sings my soul, my Savior God to
    Thee,
How great Thou art, how great Thou art."*

He reached for her hand as the last notes of the
chorus faded across the yard into the night. "While
growing up, I went to church because my parents
made me go. There comes a time, though, when
every person has to find God for himself."

"And have you found Him?" She squeezed his
fingers.

He cupped her hand between both of his. "I've
been looking for Him, but sometimes He seems really
far away." He brought her hand to his lips again like
he had earlier at the diner. "Not tonight, though. Not
while you were singing."

"Thank you," she whispered.

"I'm the one who should be thanking you."

"If you say so." She made a scoffing sound. "But
you hired me, not the other way around. You faced
off with my ex tonight, and you're going to help me
find a good lawyer. Seems to me I'm doing most of

the taking, while you do most of the giving," she concluded glumly.

"Yeah." He brushed his mouth against her hand again. "All you've done is hand me back my heart and soul. No biggie."

"Asher!" she exclaimed softly, not knowing what he was talking about.

"It's true," he insisted. "I was angry the day you showed up at the farm. Bitter. Sad. Not too optimistic about the future."

She gave a nervous chuckle. "Then I blew into your office and knocked you brutally off your feet, though Ghost has to share a little credit for that."

He grimaced at the memory. "And now I look forward to waking up every morning, just because I know you're going to be a part of my day."

"Believe me, everyone knows how stoked you are about having a new person to boss around," she teased, striving to lighten the mood between them.

"There is that." Asher waggled his brows mischievously at her.

"Don't I know it!" She grinned at him, not wanting to speed things along too quickly in their new relationship. She'd tried that before, and it had ended in disaster. From now on, she was taking the slow and cautious route to happiness.

"Well, since you're expecting the bear to growl, darlin', this is the part where I'm going to insist on a few guitar tunes before I drive you back."

"Playing in the moonlight? Yes, please!" Chuckling merrily, she tugged his hand to walk with her to the porch swing. They sat, and she opened her case so she could lift the guitar onto her lap. "What would you like to hear first?"

He named a country song. She picked out the melody and hummed a few notes. As before, Asher joined in on the chorus. "You have a fantastic voice," she sighed. "We should do this more often."

"You stick around a while in Chipper, and I just might." The possibilities swirling in his questioning gaze made her heart beat a little faster.

CHAPTER 7: HEALING OLD WOUNDS, CREATING NEW ONES

ASHER

AFTER SPENDING SUCH a magical evening with Bella, Asher couldn't have been less interested in attending the First Annual Chipper Hoedown the next morning. Assuming any single ladies at all hopped into his line at the kissing booth — and that was a very big *if* — how in the world was he supposed to keep his end of the bargain? The only woman he had any interest in kissing, at this point, was his new girlfriend.

It was one thing to play along with another one of Jade's foolish requests back when he was a single guy, but things had changed since then. He was no longer single.

Believe it or not, you're no longer single, dude. He stared in wonder at the scarred man in the mirror whose jaw he was shaving. Being Bella's boyfriend made him so stupidly happy that his brothers were going to be downright nauseated when they found out about it. He was never going to live down their ribbing over the fact that he'd hired his own girl-friend on the spot — before so much as checking her references. From the very beginning, there'd been something extraordinary about her that had reached out to him. Even in the midst of his anger, sadness, and bitterness, he'd somehow *known* that she was meant to become a part of Cassidy Farm. At the time, he hadn't realized she was additionally meant to become so important to him personally.

As he finished dressing, Asher found that he no longer cared what size of hat brim he wore or how far he canted it over his forehead. Though he knew he was going out in public today, his biggest mission was no longer how much of the scarred side of his face he could hide. Like Bella had continually reiterated to him, through her words as well as her actions, it didn't matter. It really didn't.

Like she said, people who cared about stuff like that weren't worth calling friends. And they sure as heck weren't worth kissing. Way down deep inside, he'd always known that. The only reason it had taken so long to come to grips with it was because of what had happened between him and Jade.

If he was being honest with himself, her rejection still stung. Because of their lifelong friendship, it probably always would. However, he was slowly coming to terms with that, too. It was time to move on. He owed Bella no less.

Which meant it was time to finally clear the air with Jade. They'd grown up together, their families were friends, and they had to live in the same town.

Someone had to be the first to offer an olive branch, and that someone might as well be him.

As he headed to his truck, he had to scroll through his address book to find her name. He'd long since removed her off his speed dial list, something that still managed to twang a painful chord in his chest. Grimacing at his own weakness, he mashed the call button before he changed his mind.

In true Jade style, she let it ring a long time. Since he was waiting for it to connect to his speaker system before starting to drive, it meant he was temporarily stuck sitting in his garage.

You little twit! He held the phone away from his face to scowl at the screen on the fourth ring. There was no way she didn't see him trying to call her. On a day like today, the control freak in her would have her earpiece in and the phone itself attached to her person. Was she really going to let him go to voicemail? What in heaven's name had he done to deserve such animosity from her? It was truly mind-boggling.

Right when he was convinced his call was going to voicemail, the phone stopped in mid-ring and Jade's cool voice sounded in his ear. "The answer is no."

His jaw tightened. "I haven't asked for anything yet."

"Then don't bother. You're not backing out on me at the last minute like this. I have a kissing booth to run and fire station to fund, and you Cassidys are going to do your part if it kills you."

"The Cassidys have always done their part, thank you very much."

"And you will continue to do so, if I have any say in the matter." There was no softening in her tone. She was giving up no ground.

Whatever. He drove from his garage and crunched his way down the gravel driveway to the main hub of Cassidy Farm. "I asked a girl out last night," he informed her bluntly.

"Too bad," she shot back without even the slightest hesitation. "I hope you explained to her your prior commitment to our newly incorporated town and our future fire department."

"Because you know all about keeping your commitments, eh?" The moment the words left his mouth, Asher wanted to kick himself. He hadn't called Jade to start an argument.

A shocked silence met his words. For a moment, he thought she was going to hang up on him. However, her voice finally wafted across the line again. "As a matter of fact, I do, Asher Cassidy. It's probably the only reason you and I aren't trapped in a loveless marriage right this second."

His chest constricted with pain. "That's pretty low, even for you."

"Sometimes the truth hurts, Ash. Believe me, I know what I'm talking about."

He made a sound of disbelief. "Are you trying to tell me you were the one who was hurting the day you broke up with me?"

"Not the only one," she sighed, "but I was definitely one of the two people in that equation. Yes, it hurt me, too."

"Then why did you do it?" he demanded.

"Because we weren't right for each other. And if you can ever get that through your thick skull, you'll agree that breaking up was our only viable option at that point. Our relationship had been on and off for months leading up to it. It was only a matter of time before one of us ended it."

"Your timing was pretty poor," he growled. "You made me feel damaged beyond repair. Worthless. Like nothing."

"That was never my intention," she cried shrilly. "I'll admit the timing was off. In hindsight, it was probably the worst mistake of my adult life. I should've waited longer. Given you more time to heal."

"But you were still going to break up with me."

"Yes." Her voice dropped to just barely above a whisper.

"Because you couldn't bear the thought of being saddled with a scarred and broken cowboy like—"

"Stop!" she shouted. "Just stop!"

He stopped. He stopped talking, and he stopped driving because he'd reached the parking pad beside his office.

"Please stop," she repeated in a shaky voice. "I'm going to say this one time and one time only. If you and I had loved each other, nothing would have stopped me from marrying you. No fire. No scars.

Not even a severed limb. Nothing but death would've kept me away from you."

"I did love you," he retorted hoarsely. "I really loved you, Jade."

"And I loved you," she returned. "A part of me always will. I love every single one of you Cassidys, no matter how mad y'all make me sometimes. The problem with you and me back then was we weren't *in* love. Not the way your parents are and my parents are. Not the forever and always kind of love between soul mates. If you're being honest with yourself, *really* honest, you know I'm right."

As he hunched over his steering wheel, mind racing, his gaze fell on the emerald green Jaguar parked in the circle drive in front of the main ranch house.

You've got to be kidding me! Jade was here? At Cassidy Farm?

A tap on his window had his head spinning to investigate the sound.

Jade was standing there, all dolled up like a million bucks in another one of her silk shirts. This one was as green as her car.

He cracked open his door, and she stepped back to give him room to leap to the ground. "Speak of the devil," he drawled.

"Takes one to know one," she returned, reaching up to flip back her long, strawberry blonde hair.

"Apparently, we haven't forgotten how to bicker." He firmly shut his truck door and leaned back against it, arms folded.

"Does this mean you're finally ready to forgive me?" Hugging a clipboard to her chest, she tipped her face anxiously up to his.

Asher gave the shadows beneath her eyes a hard scrutiny. "Is this your way of saying I've been acting like an idiot?"

She gave a breathless chuckle. "If the shoe fits."

"I was really hurt by the way you left." He wasn't yet finished with their conversation. "We all were."

"I am well aware." Her normally snapping green eyes grew glassy. "Your brothers have spent the entire last year scorching me with their glares and shredding me to pieces with their words."

"Why didn't you say something?" he demanded. "We were supposed to be friends."

"Would it have done any good?" She shrugged her delicate shoulders. "The damage was already done."

"You could have at least tried," he muttered, glancing away.

"I wanted to." She drew a deep breath. "I imagined a thousand different things I might say during a thousand different scenarios. I finally broke down in front of your parents and begged for their advice."

"When?" This was news to him.

"Many, many months ago." She shrugged. "Shortly after you came home from the hospital.

"What did they say?" He was curious about why they'd never mentioned it to him.

"To leave it alone. That time heals a lot of things, and God does the rest. At first, I thought it was because they hated me as much as you did. That it was just their way of pushing my horrible self as far as possible from their precious family. But I think this conversation proves they knew exactly what they were talking about."

"Maybe." Asher hadn't come into the conversation with the burning desire to admit that Jade was right about anything. However, the truth always stood on its own two feet. If Jade hadn't broken up with him, one of the most wonderful things that had ever happened to him wouldn't have happened. No way in this world would he be dating Bella Johnson right now.

Which brought him full circle to the original reason he'd reached out to Jade this morning. "Just so you know, I really did ask someone out last night."

"Let me guess." She rolled her eyes. "You've been canoodling with that new ranch hand of yours."

He scowled down at her. "That's a pretty crass way of putting it."

"I'll take that as a yes. I would know if it was one of the single ladies from around here, because I know everything there is to know about what's going on in this town." Her voice turned bitter. "But y'all Cassidys are too good to tap into the local dating pool, huh?"

He stared at her. "I have no idea what you're talking about."

"Really?" Her eyes snapped with righteous indignation. "I bet you can't tell me the last time any of your brothers asked a local girl on a date."

He lifted his Stetson to run his hand through his hair as he considered her words. Now that she mentioned it, none of his brothers had done much dating lately. Not since the fire. Asher had always assumed Fox romanced the ladies on the rodeo circuit, but he honestly hadn't ever asked. At first, he'd been too busy recovering from his injuries. After that, he'd been too busy running a ranch.

"See what I mean?" Jade waved a red-lacquered fingernail at him with an aha expression.

"Quit gloating," he growled. "It's not attractive."

She burst into laughter. "Wow! It's pretty liberating, isn't it?"

He shook his head at her. "Again, I have no idea what you're talking about."

"Putting me in my place." Still clutching her clipboard, she ticked the reasons off on her fingers. "Being honest with each other. Finally admitting some of the stuff you never liked about me in the first place. It's liberating."

Despite the fact that she was right again, he waved a hand at her in disgust. "Can we get back to the kissing booth issue?"

"Sure. You're in the number one spot in our lineup. Hope you're prepared for a considerable amount of necking this afternoon with our lovely hometown girls. And by a few, I mean dozens. Literally." Her chuckle was gleeful. "I recruited them myself."

His gaze narrowed on hers. "I never knew you were this cruel."

"Whatever long list of bad adjectives you've come to associate with me, I assure you I'm far worse." Her tone was cheeky. "Which is why I'm not letting you off the hook."

"Still not interested."

"Well, the single ladies of this town are, and it required very little effort on my part. All I did was spread the word that you were going to pucker up for us at the hoedown, and the money pledges started pouring in."

"You're missing the point, Jade." Man, she'd always been like a bulldog with a bloody bone when she sank her teeth into a project. There was no stopping her, though he sure intended to try.

"This isn't about you and me anymore, Asher. It's about what's right for the town of Chipper. It's about your sweet mama's dream of building us an all-new fire department. And it most certainly is also about the number of women who would jump at the chance to kiss you." Her voice softened on that last part.

He pointed incredulously at the damaged side of his face. "You really think anyone's gonna jump at the chance to kiss this?"

"Do you need proof, cowboy?" Before he could respond, she danced closer to him and stretched on her tiptoes to press the gentlest of kisses to his damaged cheek. "There you have it." She stepped back and pointed at her own face. "This is my not running-and-screaming-in-horror face."

The decidedly female gasp to their left was his

first clue that they had an audience. Glancing toward the sound, Asher was riveted by the sight of Bella wearing a dress again. This time it was a long and flowy beige one that brought to mind a wedding gown. A turquoise necklace circled her throat, and a split in the skirt at her knees revealed she had on her favorite cowgirl boots. No, not her favorite ones. They were new, gem-encrusted, high-heeled ones. *Holy smokes!*

Asher felt his eyes bugging out of his head. "You're so beautiful, Bella."

Jade cleared her throat from somewhere nearby. "Guess I'm not needed here anymore."

Silence fell between him and Bella as she click-clacked her way back up the sidewalk to the ranch house, presumably to meet with his parents.

"Wow. I'm not so sure I'm needed here anymore, either." Bella lifted her chin. Her cheeks had gone a ghastly shade of pale.

"What are you talking about?" Asher pushed away from his truck to stride in her direction. He wanted to take her in his arms, but something in her expression held him back.

"This isn't the first time I've walked up to a guy I'm supposed to be dating, only to find out his interests were otherwise occupied."

Asher stared at her, not comprehending at first. However, there was no denying the hurt staining Bella's features. There was a bruised cast to her eyes that made his heart ache. "Wait. You think…" He glanced back at Jade's retreating figure. "She and I are not…" He seriously couldn't believe that Bella was forcing him into the position of defending himself.

"At least this time around I wasn't already engaged." Her voice was so bitter that Asher perceived he had the start of a real problem on his hands.

"Whatever you seem to think is going on between Jade and me…isn't," he protested.

"You kissed," she pointed out dully.

Asher shook his head. "Actually, she did the kissing, and it was only on the cheek. All I did was stand there."

"All you did was stand there, huh? While the woman who supposedly broke your heart a year ago had her mouth in the same place mine was last night. If I'm not supposed to have an opinion about that, my bad. Because I do," Bella stormed. Two angry red spots replaced the whiteness in her cheeks.

"Nothing happened. I promise."

"How can you say that?" Bella sounded close to weeping. "Jade, of all people in the world, just got close enough to kiss you, so you might want to rethink your story. Something most definitely happened between the two of you. And until you figure out exactly what that is, I no longer wish to be a part of this." She gestured between the two of them.

His eyebrows shot heavenward. "Are you breaking up with me?" His hand flew to the top of his hat as disbelief shot through him.

"Yeah." Her eyes might as well have been shooting brown flames. "I think I am. I've been in this position before, so I am all too familiar with how un-cool it is to be the other woman in a man's life."

"Bella, please!" He couldn't have been more exasperated. "The whole reason I reached out to Jade was to tell her that I'm dating you, so I can't participate in the kissing booth today."

"Right." Bella's eyes narrowed to dangerously narrow slits. "That's all this was ever about, wasn't it? Using me as a human shield to keep you from getting the thin skin around your heart blistered all over again."

"No!" Well… "Okay, maybe it started out that way." He knew he sounded like the world's biggest fool, but he didn't care. "Then I kissed you. Afterward, I lost interest in kissing anyone else, so help me God."

"Until this morning," Bella noted bitterly. "What really happened between you and Jade? Because from the looks of things, I'm guessing you two finally patched things up."

"We did." He blew out a frustrated breath. "We finally said some things that needed to be said and—"

"I'm happy for you, Asher." Bella's voice was still thick with hurt. "That's how stupid I am. I care enough about you that I'm actually happy for you."

He gazed longingly down at her. "I'd be a lot happier if you'd just get in the truck already. I came to drive you to the hoedown."

"I have a different ride lined up."

"Since when?"

Fox chose that moment to stride out of the barn with Ghost at his heels.

"Hey, Fox!" Bella called without dropping Asher's gaze. "Mind giving me a lift to the hoedown?"

"Sure. No problem, beautiful."

"See? I have a ride." She pinched her lips together.

Fox paused as he drew abreast of them, head swiveling between the two of them. "Whoa! What's going on?"

"Nothing," Bella said coolly. "Absolutely nothing."

Asher's brain froze as she pivoted away from him and stooped to pet Ghost. In response to Fox's questioning look, he waved a hand. "Just take her," he growled.

He leaped inside his truck and slammed the door shut. Then he revved his motor and roared off, spinning far more gravel than was necessary. He knew he was being a jerk, but he didn't care. What just happened back there between him and Bella felt a dozen shades of unfair. He hadn't even been given the chance to properly explain himself.

Pounding his fists against the steering wheel, he shouted into the empty cab, "She didn't even give me a chance to explain!" A groan escaped him at the realization that he sounded all too much like Jim Steering had last night, which didn't make him feel any better. What a bloody mess!

He arrived at the rodeo grounds in another spray of gravel, yanked his truck up the nearest row, and jammed his brakes into the first parking spot at the end. Leaping to the ground, he slammed his door shut without locking it and stomped toward the area of the stadium that Jade had described.

Though it was a full hour before starting time, the place was already crammed full of townsfolk. Some were scurrying to move food and beverage kiosks into place. Others were setting up the dance floor in the center of the ring. There would be square dancing, swing dancing, and heaven only knew what else. Jade had advertised it like a dance off. Couples would pay a fee to enter, or friends could sponsor them. A panel of judges would select winners in various categories, and prizes would be distributed. All profits from the event would go toward funding the new fire department.

Beldon, Cormac, and the twins were already there at the kissing booth, a side event that would start for an hour in the morning and resume for a few hours in the afternoon. Various single hopeful ladies were simpering over his brothers, straightening their collars and adjusting their bolos.

Beldon took one look at Asher and held up his hand for the woman in front of him to pause her fussing. "Be right back."

He strode toward his oldest brother and angled his head away from the group. "Walk with me."

Not sure what else to do, Asher fell into step beside him.

"You look like the world is coming to an end. What gives?" Beldon's scowl was probably a mirror image of the one Asher was currently wearing. They looked enough alike to pass as twins. They weren't identical, but they were close — minus the scars, of course. Beldon had gotten their dad's brown eyes, while Asher had gotten their mom's blue ones, but both had their father's brown hair, angular features, and rigid work ethic. Both poured one hundred percent of their time and energy into the family business — Asher as their ranch manager and Beldon as their chief range rider who tended the herds.

"I blew it, Beldon. I really blew it this time." Asher was still reeling on the inside, trying to figure out what he could've done to avoid the shambles he was currently wallowing in.

"I'm going to need more details than that, bro."

Nodding, Asher disclosed the grim state of things between him and Bella. As he spoke, Beldon's expression grew more thunderous. "I can't believe Jade has struck again!" he snarled. "That woman blazes a trail of destruction everywhere she goes. When you saw her walking your way, you should've run."

Asher shrugged, a little surprised by his brother's level of vehemence. "She was already there. Guess I should've never called her on the phone. I should've just not shown up today." He gripped his hat with both hands. "The real problem is this. How do I make it up to Bella? I don't want to lose her, Beldon. I can't." The very thought made his chest ache.

Beldon studied him shrewdly. "You really care for her."

"I do."

"Are you in love with her?"

"Don't know yet. We just started dating. Man, Beldon! How did this happen?" Asher spun around to walk backwards. "To me, of all people!"

Beldon's scowl deepened. "What's that supposed to mean?"

"Oh, come on!" Asher waved in irritation at his scars. "How does a hideous guy like me come down with women problems?"

"Beats me." Beldon shook his head. "Maybe because women are nothing but trouble."

Again, his vehemence surprised Asher. "Then why did you agree to work at the kissing booth?"

"Same as you." Beldon slung a light punch at his shoulder. "I was voluntold. Mom is serious about that fire department, and I think we all know why."

Asher snorted and fell back into step beside him. "She'd pack me in bubble wrap if she could."

"So, let's get back there and get the kissing booth shenanigans over with, shall we?"

"There's only one problem with that," Asher groaned. Actually, there were a lot of problems with it, though one stood out more than the others. "I don't want to kiss anyone besides Bella. I know she broke up with me, but my heart is far from single and available." It still belonged to her.

"Then prove it to her."

"How?" Asher was fresh out of ideas. His brain felt like mush.

"I don't know. Wing it until you think of something." Beldon's jaw tightened. "The only advice I've got is this. If you really care about Bella, stick to your guns and don't kiss any other females besides her. No matter what."

"Okay." Asher ran his hand over his jaw. "Okay."

CHAPTER 8: KISSING BOOTH CONUNDRUM

BELLA

BELLA STARED out the window as Fox drove. He was the proud owner of a juiced-up off-roading vehicle he'd essentially built out of spare parts from the salvage yard. It had roll bars, extra lights on top, a bazillion aerials, and a new camouflage paint job. She felt like she was riding inside a tank. Though it was only a five-minute trip to the stadium, the strained silence in the air made it feel just shy of forever.

"You gonna tell me what's going on over there?" Fox finally asked.

"Don't ask." She wrapped her arms around her middle. It was all she could do not to weep.

"Already did," he announced cheerfully.

"Why do you have to sound so stinking happy about everything all the time?" she grumbled.

"Because you can't hide this kind of sunshine," he teased.

"Oh, give me a break," she muttered.

"Hey, you're the one who asked for a ride. That means you get to put up with my choice of radio stations along with my fascinating commentary about life in general. And right now, you happen to be the most fascinating thing I have to commentate on."

"Yay me!" She chuckled despite her efforts to hang on to her mad.

"I knew you'd come around if I explained it to you," he shot back. Then he sobered. "Seriously, Bells. Whatever's wrong between you and Ash, you gotta fix it. We almost lost him before. I don't want to lose him again."

She rigidly turned away from the window, allowing her gaze to flicker to his. "Don't put that on me. It's not fair."

"I don't care what you call it. It's true." Concern was etched across his handsome features. "I haven't seen my oldest brother this happy in a long time, and you're the only one I can blame for that. He changed because of you. I was just starting to feel like I got him back, and now this." He threw his hands in the air.

"Put your hands back on the steering wheel," she squeaked. "You're supposed to be driving."

"It doesn't take hands to drive, beautiful." Instead of returning his callused fingers to the steering wheel, he propped one jean-clad knee beneath it to steer. A lock of his dark, longish hair fell across his forehead as he drove. Before taking off, he'd tossed his Stetson between them on the console.

"Fox!"

He returned his hands to the wheel. "Did you say something?"

"Just…drive." She turned back to the window.

"You know you care about him," he pressed.

"I said just drive."

"He definitely cares about you."

"He has a funny way of showing it," she snapped.

"You knew he was a crab when you agreed to come to work for him."

"I'm referring to the fact that he let Jade kiss him this morning," she explained through gritted teeth.

"What?" Fox mashed on his brakes and yanked his vehicle to the shoulder. "What did you say?"

"You heard me." She squeezed her eyes shut.

"Jade? As in Jade Witch-and-a-Half Arletta?"

"The one and only," she concurred tiredly.

"No way! I'm not buying it."

"I saw it with my own eyes," she insisted.

"What exactly did you see?"

"She kissed him on the cheek." Bella blinked back tears at the memory.

"On the cheek, huh?" Fox made a sound of derision. "That's it?"

"Right on top of his scars." She sniffled loudly. "Right in the same spot where I kissed him last night."

Fox was silent for a moment. "So, uh, correct me if I'm wrong, but I'm betting you kissed my brother in a few other spots last night, as well."

Hot tears streaked down her cheeks, and a whimper of misery escaped her.

"Did he kiss her back?"

"He didn't do anything from what I could tell. He just stood there with his arms crossed."

Fox's look was disbelieving. "Doesn't sound to me like he was that into her kiss."

The first curls of shame unfurled in her chest. "All I saw was Jim Steering cheating on me all over again," she sobbed. "Unless you've ever experienced that kind of pain, don't even pretend you know how it feels."

"You're right. I don't," Fox snarled. "After meeting your ex last night, one thing was clear. He's an A-class dirtbag. Asher isn't. If my brother's arms stayed folded during this kiss that has you so worked up, I can assure you there's nothing for you to worry about. If he was interested in that sorry excuse for a woman, his hands would've been a lot more occupied. Kind of like they were with you last night. I don't think he stopped touching you the whole time I was there at the diner. It was truly gag-worthy. He's into you, Bells. *Really* into you."

She smiled through her tears, though another jagged sob worked its way up her throat. "So, what you're trying to say is, I shouldn't get even with him by blowing my entire first paycheck from Cassidy Farm at the kissing booth today."

He sent her an incredulous look. "You do realize it's us Cassidy brothers manning the booth?"

She nodded, chuckling damply. "I was actually thinking of buying one kiss from each of you."

He wrinkled his nose in distaste. "Feeling awfully charitable today, are you?"

"Apparently, I'm not that good of a person." She shook her head. "I was mostly imagining the best ways to make steam come out of Asher's ears." She balled her fists as she wailed, "He makes me so mad sometimes, Fox!"

He grinned. "Sounds like the makings of true love to me."

"True lo—oh, my gosh! Did you hear a word I said? I'm so mad at him right now, I could scream!"

"Yeah, I heard you, and now it's your turn to hear me." He pulled back onto the road. "I adore you to pieces, Bells, and so does Ghost. But don't even think about slapping money down in front of the spot where I'm sitting. It would feel like I was kissing my sister."

"You don't have any sisters," she pointed out reasonably.

"Yet," he retorted with a sly glance at her.

She blushed. "Just so you know, I broke up with Asher already." She thought she was finished crying, but another sob tore its way from her.

"Then un-break up with him, for crying out loud. This isn't some quickie high school fling. This is about his future happiness and yours." Fox paused to purse his lips thoughtfully. "And mine, since I have to put up with all of y'all."

"You *would* find a way of making this about you." She sent him a dark look.

He gestured at his steering wheel. "Am I not right smack in the middle of this?"

"Okay, okay," she cajoled. "You may have a point."

"May?" He sounded taken aback.

"So, how can I make this right, Fox?" Now that the worst bite of Bella's anger was wearing off, no small amount of shame was setting in. No matter what angle she looked at the situation from, Fox was right. She'd most likely misread the situation between Asher and Jade and wa-a-a-ay overreacted.

"Well, since you asked so nicely…" He cast a cagey glance her way.

"Uh-oh. I'm not going to like what you're about to say, am I?"

"Not sure why you jumped to that conclusion." He drummed his fingers on the wheel. "I was just thinking."

"Again. Uh-oh."

He ignored her. "All that money you were planning on blowing on the wrong brothers, why not blow it on Asher, instead? The whole wad!"

She felt her face heat. "Um, I just finished saying some pretty tough stuff to him. What if I've ruined things between us so bad that he doesn't want me to kiss him?"

"Good gravy, Bells! If you're going to be a couple, you're going to screw up things now and then. It's part of the package deal. That's what make-up kisses are for."

She studied him curiously. "You sound particularly well-versed on the topic of kissing and making up. Exactly how many women have you made mad?"

"Too many." He started to whistle. "That's probably why I'm still single."

"You don't sound very upset about your single state."

"Because I'm not." He waggled his eyebrows playfully at her. "Some guys are born to be single."

"I don't believe that for one second, especially not about you." She leaned over to lightly whack his shoulder. "There's someone for everyone out there."

He shrugged. "Then maybe I just haven't met her yet. Either way, I'm going to enjoy manning my end of the kissing booth today. Asher, on the other hand, will not. Take my word for it. You've spoiled him for any other woman. So, have a little mercy on him, will you?"

Bella definitely liked the idea of sharing a few make-up kisses with Asher so much more than exacting revenge on him via his brothers. Shame filled her at the fact she'd even considered doing something so dastardly. If she'd followed through with it, she'd be no better than Jim. Or Jade, for that matter. The woman had caused so much trouble for the Cassidys, it was a wonder she had the gall to continue showing her face in their town.

Fox pulled into the grassy parking lot outside the

stadium and nosed his vehicle next to a familiar black truck on one of the end rows. Bella's heartbeat quickened to note that it was Asher's truck.

She sucked in a breath. "I'm glad he made it here safely." He'd been pretty mad when he drove away. Entirely her fault, of course. She rubbed her hands over her face. "I'm so not ready to face him again."

Fox jogged around to her side of his off-roading rig to help her down. "Well, you look ready. You're so pretty that I can't think straight when I'm looking at you."

"I thought you said you only had brotherly feelings for me."

"Maybe I lied."

"Fox!" she moaned.

"Okay, fine. I'm kidding." He pointed both fingers at her. "But I did manage to put some color back in your face. You're welcome. Now go get 'em, beautiful!" He clapped his hands twice.

"I'm not a dog." She made a face at him. "You don't have to clap to get me moving."

"Somebody tell that to Ghost, please." He reached around her to retrieve his Stetson and clap it back on his head. "He doesn't listen to one thing I say or do. Just does what he wants."

"Typical guy," she teased.

"Hey!" He glared ferociously down at her. "I resemble that remark."

"Don't I know it!"

As they shared a chuckle, he tossed an arm

around her shoulders. Then he steered her across the grassy field to the fast-filling stadium.

As they moved closer to the entrance gates, panic shot through her. "I don't know if I can do this," she choked.

"Sure you can." His arm settled more heavily on her shoulders, as if to make sure she didn't make a run for it.

"Seriously, Fox. I'm dying on the inside. Part of me wants to turn around and start running," she confessed breathlessly. "I want to run, run, run and never look back."

"Well, you'll just have to swallow the feeling, even if it gags you," he said flatly. "There aren't many women in the world I'd want as sisters, and now that I've found one, I'm not about to let you go."

She gave a nervous laugh. "There you go again, making this all about you."

"Nope. Not entirely." He suddenly bent down to kiss her cheek. "Just not going to let you forget the part that does include me."

"Okay. You win this round, cowboy. I'll try to talk to Asher. There are no guarantees it's going to work, but I'll at least try. And if it doesn't work, then I'll run."

"You won't get very far if you try, because I suspect Asher's not going to let you run. But that's just my opinion." He hugged her again before letting her go. Then he gave her a gentle nudge. "There's the kissing booth, and there's Asher. Go get 'em, tiger."

CHAPTER 9: NO RISK, NO REWARDS

ASHER

THE KISSING booth made Asher think of a row of horse stalls, but smaller. There were six alcoves built with two by four wooden boards. Two chairs rested side-by-side in each alcove. A Cassidy brother was stationed inside, each one with an empty chair sitting next to him. The empty chairs were for the single ladies who would pay to kiss them, assuming Jade was telling the truth about recruiting a whole army of them.

White and pale pink roses intertwined with greenery were draped over the top of the alcoves. The sign nailed to the center of it got right to the point. It read *$100 Per Kiss*. About twenty feet or so in front of the alcoves was the cashier's table, where Jade Arletta sat.

Asher stared a hole between her slender shoulder blades, incensed at her all over again for ruining his happiness. At first, it had felt good to air their feelings to each other after all this time — to finally engage in a real conversation. It was a relief to begin the repair work on such an old, longstanding friendship, a patch job for which both of their families would be grateful. Then she'd gone and ruined things between them all over again by kissing him. That was Jade, though. She was a go-big-or-go-home kind of gal. Always had been, always would be. She was one of those women you would love or hate, but it was next to impossible to feel anything for her in between those two emotions. She was that extreme, that unpredictable.

"I really despise her right now," Beldon muttered to no one in particular in the next alcove over.

Asher didn't have to ask who he was talking about. Though he silently agreed with the sentiment, he didn't see how talking about it would change anything. What mattered right now was preparing for his forthcoming confrontation with Bella. In his gut, he felt like he was going to get one shot, and one shot only. Otherwise, she might very well hit the road again before nightfall.

Asher's mother walked up to them. "My lands, y'all! This is a hoedown, not a funeral." She was wearing a frothy square-dancing dress with many layers of petticoats. Pausing in front of Asher, she reached for his hands. "I love you so much for doing this."

"If you say it's for a good cause one more time, I'm going to puke." Fox's mutter from the end of the row was loud enough to carry down to her.

Her merry laugh lightened some of the heaviness

in Asher's chest. "Then I won't." Her laughter faded as she took in their expressions. "Something's wrong. I can feel it."

"We're fine, Mom. Just looking forward to watching you and Dad rock it on the dance floor." For reasons Asher hadn't understood until his conversation earlier with Jade, she and Jade had remained friends. So it made no sense to share with his mother the latest round of wounds Jade had inflicted on him.

"Where's Bella?" his mother asked suddenly. As she moved her head from side to side to take in their surroundings, her dyed blonde hair swung girlishly against her shoulders. Even though she was pushing fifty, she was still a beautiful woman. She always would be, because she was one of those people who was as beautiful on the inside as she was on the outside. "I saw her speaking with that television reporter a few minutes ago," she mused. "He's going around to all the single ladies, asking them if they're going to visit the kissing booth and trying to build the buzz for more donations."

Television? Asher sat up straighter as a crazy thought struck him. "Any idea which television station it was?"

"No. All I know is they're from Amarillo," she supplied vaguely. "Don't worry. You'll get to meet them. Jade made sure they knew about the kissing booth." She lifted her hand and waved excitedly to someone on the outdoor dance floor. "There's your Dad. Gotta scoot."

As Asher mulled over his mother's limited information concerning the television crew, he'd never before wanted so badly to strangle his ex. Jade hadn't liked Bella from the start. And now she thought she was going to have a television station record Bella's boyfriend kissing a slew of other women to further humiliate her. *Over my dead body!* Asher leaped to his feet as the idea in his head blossomed to a full-blown plan. Enough was enough.

"Down, boy!" Beldon called quietly.

Asher didn't answer. Instead, he strode up to Jade's table. "New plan," he announced coldly. "You will return the money of anyone who pays to kiss me, and I'll match it with a donation of my own."

She glanced up at him in surprise. "That's not how this works."

"It is now." He rapped his knuckles on her table. "Either you agree to my terms, or I'm gone."

"Asher!" she protested, looking doubtful.

He slapped his hands down on the table to bring them eye level, making her jump. "Spare me the lecture. Nobody around here is impressed with words. What they want is a little action." He whipped out his wallet and waved five hundred dollars in the air. Then he slapped it down on the table and turned around to face the line of single ladies that was forming. "I'll be starting off this event with a five hundred dollar donation. That's worth five kisses. And since I have no interest in kissing my own brothers," his words were met with a round of laughter, "I hereby nominate our fearless committee chairperson, Jade Arletta, to do the honors."

A round of applause met his announcement.

She stared up at him in growing consternation. Before she could come up with a cutting response, he leaned closer and growled, "In case you're wondering, that's what it feels like to have someone interfere in your life. So buckle up and enjoy a taste of your own medicine." As he moved around her table to stomp back to his chair, he nearly collided with Bella.

"Hey, darlin'." Without thinking, he cupped her shoulders to steady her, scowling in concern. It was so good to see her again that his brain went blank for a moment. All he could feel was blind joy and the painful sting of longing, mostly longing.

"That was pretty harsh." She glanced past his shoulder with something akin to sympathy for Jade.

"She deserved it." He clenched his jaw. "She's nothing but a troublemaker."

"Maybe." She returned her gaze to his to scan his features anxiously. "Asher, we need to talk."

His heart pitched crazily at her words. The fact that she wanted to talk was a very good sign that he hadn't permanently ruined things between them.

"Yeah, we do," he agreed, "and there's no maybe about it when it comes to Jade Arletta." Keeping his hands on her shoulders, he led her back to his alcove in the kissing booth and gently nudged her into the chair beside his. "She's done more harm than she'll ever understand to me, my family, and my girlfriend."

"You've got a girlfriend?" Bella pretended surprise as she swiveled to face him. "The way we left things, I'm pretty sure makes you single again."

"I don't feel single."

"Asher," she murmured in a voice choked with emotion. "What am I going to do with you?"

"I'm really hoping you'll take me back." He reached for her hand and laced his fingers through hers, unable to tear his gaze away from her. "I'll beg if you want me to."

Tears gathered in her eyes.

He felt a little like crying himself. "You're still beautiful, by the way, even when you're mad at me."

"About that," she sighed. "I may have overreacted just a teensy bit."

Relief flooded him at the remorse in her voice. "I'm not so sure that you did. Someone should slug me for letting Jade come anywhere near me." He bent to press his forehead to hers. "After I had a chance to replay in my head what you had to witness between me and her, your reaction made a lot more sense. If our roles had been reversed, I wouldn't have taken it half as well."

"You didn't ask her to kiss you." Bella reached up to cup his scarred cheek.

The possessiveness of her touch made his heart sing. *That's right, darlin', I'm yours.*

"I doubt you even saw it coming," she continued in a rueful voice.

"You're right. I didn't. I was too busy trying to renegotiate the terms of this blasted kissing booth."

"I think you succeeded." She leaned back to offer him a smile brimming with cautious hope. "I heard what you said to Jade about matching the donations in your line. Does that mean what I think it means?"

"That I don't plan to kiss anyone besides you ever again? Yes, darlin', it does."

Her gaze grew all soft and vulnerable. "If that's the case, I hope you don't mind that I called in a few reinforcements."

"Reinforcements?" He was so busy eyeing her with curiosity that he didn't immediately notice the camera crew moving closer to them.

"Good morning from Chipper, Texas," the announcer crowed into his microphone. "Meet Bella Johnson and her boyfriend, Asher Cassidy, a real-life hero who ran into a burning barn last year to rescue the horses trapped inside their stalls. At the time, the community he lived in didn't have their own fire department, but they're trying to change that with the funds they're raising at today's charity hoedown." His cameraman briefly fanned away his zoom lens as he launched into a description of the hoedown as a whole. Then he swung the camera back to Asher and Bella. "This is how every one of you who's listening right now can get involved and help make the new Chipper Fire Department a reality." He went on to describe Asher's dilemma of being tasked to serve in a kissing booth right after asking Bella to become his girlfriend.

"She's an out of work school teacher," the news anchor continued, "making ends meet by serving as a ranch hand at the renowned Cassidy Farm, and she's told me there's absolutely no way she's going to be able to afford to kiss Asher as many times as she wants to today. What's worse, when her money runs out, other single ladies will be able to pull out their wallets to purchase the right to kiss her man. That hardly seems fair to these brand spanking new love-birds, does it? Which is where you come in. For every one hundred dollars we raise in donations, Bella will be able to give the man she loves one more kiss. So, what do you say about lending them a hand? All you've gotta do is pick up the phone and call this number." He rattled it off a few times for the benefit of his listeners.

As the camera panned away to the dancers once again in the center of the stadium, Asher stared at Bella, utterly stunned. "I can't believe you did this for me." It was the most incredible thing anyone had ever done for him.

She raised and lowered her shoulders as she drenched him with a tremulous smile. "Drastic times call for drastic measures. By now, you've probably figured out how I feel about having to stand by and watch other women kissing you."

"You're incredible, Bella Johnson." The fact that she'd been roused to such a display of jealousy could only mean one thing. She truly cared about him.

"I was told by a certain youngest brother of yours that make-up kisses can be pretty incredible," she whispered.

Unable to hold back a second longer, Asher

reached out to run his thumb along the perfect curve of her perfectly rosy lower lip. *Fox, you may have finally redeemed yourself, bro.* He wished he and Bella were anywhere besides a stadium full of gawking townsfolk. The way he wanted to kiss her right now needed no audience.

"I love you, Bella." His voice was rough with emotion.

"Asher!" she gasped, blushing to the roots of her dark, silky hair.

"You once said that everything was running together about what was real and not real between us, and that I was supposed to help you sort everything out when it was all over." He gazed at her with his heart in his eyes. "So, here's the thing. It's never going to be over between us, because it's all real."

With a sobbing squeal of happiness, she threw her arms around his neck. "Do you really mean it, Asher?"

"With all of my heart." He crushed his mouth to hers.

She gave a soft sigh that tugged every piece of his heart closer to hers. A dizzy brand of joy blossomed between them, along with a peace he'd never experienced before. Their kisses had never felt this good, either. What was happening between them was no mistake. It was everything that was right and real. The lasting kind of love.

Asher never wanted to stop kissing her, but eventually he had to come up for air. When he tried to dive back in for a second kiss, however, she pulled back out of kissing range, laughing joyfully.

"I only paid two hundred dollars to buy a little time for the television station to do its thing," she informed him breathlessly.

His gaze dropped hungrily to her mouth. "So, I only get two kisses to start off with?"

"It's all my measly budget can spare, so take your time and make this second one last, cowboy."

He cuddled her against his chest. "I'm sorry about what happened earlier." He'd be extra careful in the future. Life was too short, and Bella was too precious to him.

"I'm the only one who needs to apologize." Her well-kissed lips curved into a wobbly smile. "I jumped to the wrong conclusions."

"But you did it for the right reasons," he interjected huskily. "Believe me, I'm more than okay with that." He shook his head in wonder. "Never thought I'd be capable of inspiring that kind of jealousy in any woman." It had caught him off guard and emotionally rocked him back on his heels.

"Well, you are very, very capable, so go easy on my heart. Please."

"I'm going to ask the same of you," he dipped his head over hers to bring their mouths closer, "because I'm starting to think that my heart won't survive long without you. I want you in my life, Bella. I need you in it."

"I love you so much, Asher!" Closing the distance

between them, she fused her lips to his again for their second kiss.

It was worth so much more than a hundred dollars to him. In that moment, there was nothing he wouldn't have paid, nothing he wouldn't have given to receive it.

"Well, folks!" the television announcer boomed from somewhere nearby. "I'm happy to report that the donations are pouring in for Asher and Bella, which is a very good thing, because this special couple can't seem to stop kissing. And from the amount of funds we've received so far, they're not going to have to for a very long time."

———

Jade couldn't believe what a disaster her well-planned charity event was unraveling into. She was furious with her former fiancé for putting her on the spot like this in front of their growing audience. Between the kisses he'd purchased on her behalf and the hovering television, she felt like she was losing control.

"Jade! Jade! Jade!" the onlookers chanted, urging her to accept the challenge he'd thrown down.

Considering the whole event was for charity, she didn't see how she had much choice but to play along. It didn't mean she had to like it, though. *You're a heartless beast, Asher Cassidy.*

However, he wasn't the man she was most worried about right now. To buy herself a little time before she had to face her biggest nemesis again, she stood and walked toward Fox's end of the kissing booth first.

The single ladies in line at the cashier table burst into claps and cheers of encouragement as they perceived that she was accepting Asher's challenge at last.

Fox eyed her with a curled lip as she approached him. "Don't suppose there's any way out of this?"

"Yes," she snapped. "Just kiss me and get it over with."

"Well, now," he drawled, sounding so bored out of his mind that it hurt her feelings. "I've never been a big fan of rushing things with the ladies."

"Save it, windbag." Feeling close to tears, she slid her miserable self into the chair next to him and tugged his head down to hers without any further ado. Then she gave him a light peck on the lips. "There. All done, and you even lived to talk about it. And talk and talk and talk," she added sarcastically, hating the sting of tears that sprang to her eyes. She lowered her lashes before he could see them.

"Got it, ice princess. Loud and clear." He sounded so amused at her expense, that she stood and moved to Emerson's alcove in the middle of his blustering.

Jade made quick work of kissing the Cassidy twins and Cormac. There was no point in drawing out her humiliation any longer than necessary. They sat there in accusing silence, enduring her attention without comment, which was even worse than all their biting words combined in the year leading up to this moment. She could only hope that Beldon would allow her to give him a quick peck on the lips and be done with the whole distasteful business, just like his younger brothers had.

She moved into the chair next to him. "Hey, Beldon." She glanced longingly back toward the cashier's table. One more kiss to go. Then she would be a free woman again.

"Eyes over here, Jade," he returned coolly. "You're going to look at me and be present for what's coming."

"Don't make this any harder than it has to be," she pleaded.

"I'm just giving my brother his money's worth," he returned in a steely voice.

"This isn't one hundred percent my fault, you know," she reminded. "There are others who share in the blame." Him, for instance. She was no longer talking about what Asher had done today, and they both knew it. She was talking about what had happened a year ago.

In all of her wildest imagining, Jade had never intended to fall for the next younger brother of the man she was supposed to be dating. She and Beldon literally had nothing in common. Of all the Cassidy brothers, she'd spent the least amount of time talking to him and hanging out with him while they were growing up. But in the end, it hadn't mattered. His face was the only one that visited her in her dreams each night. His lips were the only lips she continued to feel against hers as strongly as if they'd been branded there with a hot iron. She could find no logical explanation for it. Their kiss had been nothing more than a foolish, ill-advised demonstration of weakness. She often wondered if she'd imagined its potency. She'd wondered if another kiss would be all it would take to cancel the torturous and never-ending cycle of longing to experience it again.

"I didn't ask for this, Jade," he reminded.

"Neither did I, Beldon. Who knows?" she countered loftily. "Maybe our first kiss, which was very much a mistake, was also a fluke. Maybe we've been worrying all this time for nothing."

Beldon's handsome features turned dark with speculation. "If you truly believe I spent the entire last year of my life worrying about one stupid kiss, then you don't know me at all. So get on over here and do your worst."

Fear and apprehension washed over her. The hurt came next. Since he'd insisted on her looking at him when she kissed him, there was no way she could hide it.

"I did worry, Beldon Cassidy," she murmured in a shaky voice. "Maybe you're too hard-hearted to feel anything for me in return, but I worried so much about the way your kiss made me feel that I immediately broke things off with the guy I was dating at the time. I risked more than you will ever understand — two families that I love more than my own life, my relationship with your brother, my friendship with you, my reputation, my happiness, and my heart."

His answering smile held no warmth. "Is that

why you flew to Europe the next day and stayed there for a full month?"

The fact that he even remembered what she'd done next totally floored her. "I'd rather discuss my reasons for coming back." She swayed dizzily in her chair. "I didn't want to, but I couldn't stay away. I had to know."

He shrugged, his hard mouth twisting bitterly. "Know what?"

"If it was real. If any of this is real." Keeping her eyes wide open, she slowly tipped her face up to his.

Though an inexplicable emotion flared in his expression, he made no effort to meet her halfway. Clearly, he was in no hurry to give her the answer she sought any sooner than he had to. He made her come all the way to him. Only when her lips touched his did his rigid posture change.

His callused hand threaded through her hair, cupping the back of her neck to pull her closer as he took what she offered. He slanted his mouth over hers and took and took and took until there was nothing in the world left but her and him.

His scent, his touch, his taste.

He wanted this as much as she did. She wanted so much more than one more kiss, though. She wanted it all, everything they'd lost — their friendship, their good opinion of each other, their mutual respect, their quiet conversations, and the rare moments of happiness that two people feel when their hearts touch.

As quickly as he'd claimed her mouth, Beldon

relinquished it. He drew back, his dark eyes burning into hers.

"You felt it, too," she whispered, silently begging him not to deny it. "I know you did."

His hard mouth twisted. "It doesn't matter."

"It does to me."

"It doesn't to me."

She caught her breath as the icy finality of his words washed over her. This was his way of saying goodbye, and it hurt every bit as much as it had the last time. No, if such a thing was even possible, it hurt more.

"You can make me feel, but you can never make me act on those feelings."

She flinched as if he'd slapped her.

———

As Jade stood and smoothed her hands over her designer jeans, Beldon tried to ignore the regret that filled him at the hurt in her eyes, knowing he was solely responsible for it this time. However, she'd been unmercifully cruel to his brother, a cruelty that had been felt by his entire family. His own ensuing suffering had been no less than excruciating. She deserved nothing but cruelty in return.

It didn't matter that what she'd made him feel was real. It didn't matter that they'd both felt it. The biggest punishment he could give her was the promise that neither of them was ever going to be allowed to feel it again.

CHAPTER 10: TANGLED WEBS

BELLA

THE FIRST ANNUAL Chipper Hoedown was supposed to end mid-afternoon, but the festivities were still in full swing come dinner time. Since most of the citizens had known each other their entire lives, they did what good friends and families often do. They pulled out leftovers.

The BBQ grills were fired back up, and the crock-pots were turned back on. What remained of the chili cook-off from lunch was soon sizzling again. It was a farm community, so new briskets appeared over the fire, along with fresh steaks, burgers, and bratwurst. Long strips of vegetables were sliced, marinated, and sautéed right next to the meat.

The contests were ended, the kissing booth closed, and the record number of donations long since counted, yet the dance floor was still far from empty. As bellies became full, more couples slipped away from the eating tents and joined those who were dipping and swaying out in the ring.

As twilight fell, the strains of country music grew slower and sweeter.

Bella slid her arms around Asher's neck and held him like she was never going to let him go. Gosh, but she loved her cowboy boss! Her partner in crime, the guy she bickered with the most, and her best friend in the universe.

As they gently rocked back and forth in time to the music, he bent to nuzzle his way from her chin to her earlobe. "Remember when I said I didn't know if I was the right guy for you, but I wanted to be?"

"Yes." She smiled at the memory. It seemed so long ago, even though it wasn't.

"I'm sure now, darlin', that I'm very much the right guy for you."

"Yes," she whispered. "You most certainly are." All her remaining doubts were gone.

He fell silent as he reached down and dug inside the pocket of his jeans for something. The next thing she knew, he was fiddling with it near her shoulder. She felt the brush of paper against her neck and then the ticklish drag of a stick or something across the sensitive skin covering her collarbone.

She gave a breathy chuckle. "What are you doing?"

"Writing," he admitted sheepishly.

"You're kidding." She chuckled again, twisting her head in an attempt to see what he was doing.

"Hold still, please. A few minutes ago, a prospective new vendor gave me his number, and I'm going to forget it if I don't write it down."

"Is that so, Mr. Ranch Manager? Right in the middle of us having a moment," she teased.

"Pleading for a little mercy here, darlin'." He stopped what he was doing to capture her mouth in a tender kiss. "No matter how much my job demands of me, you'll always come first, always be the woman I love."

"Better." She cocked her head at him. "Okay. It's my turn to write a note. Gimme." She reached up to take the pad of sticky notes and pen from his hand.

"One sec." He quickly removed the top sheet and stuffed it in the pocket of his jeans before relinquishing the items to her.

She swiftly wrote out her message and removed the note from the pad.

"What does yours say?" he demanded as she returned the other two items.

"You'll see," she promised, standing on her tiptoes to press her lips to his again.

———

He promptly forgot everything but the magic of being in her embrace. "I love you, Bella."

"I love you, too." She wrapped her arms around his neck again and they stood there together, just breathing in the joy of holding each other and being held in return.

It wasn't until they were walking in a cluster with his brothers toward the parking lot, much later, that he remembered her note.

"Are you ever going to tell me what you wrote earlier?" He bent to give her a quick kiss on the cheek.

Before she could answer, Beldon drew alongside him and bumped none too gently against his shoulder.

"Hey! What's that on the back of your shirt?"

"No idea. Don't have eyes behind my head."

In the next moment, a punch against Asher's shoulder sent his Stetson flying.

"What in the—?"

"Just doing what we're told, big guy." A punch in his other shoulder sent him reeling to the other side. He had to do a quick dance to regain his footing. He found himself facing Cormac, who was walking backwards across the parking lot. He slapped his right fist into his left hand like a boxer warming up.

"Someone care to read me in on the joke?" Asher growled, hunkering into a defensive tackle position. Out of the corner of his eye, he watched Bella back away as his other brothers converged on him from both sides.

"Who said we're joking?" Beldon gave him an unholy grin in the twilight, clearly enjoying himself. "Did anyone tell a joke? Because if you did, I missed it."

"That makes two of us," Asher snarled, swinging his head from side to side in the attempt to keep an eye on all of his brothers at the same time. It proved to be an impossible task.

Devlin circled behind him and immediately burst

into loud guffaws. "Considering the fact that you're the one who hired Bella and demanded we fall in line with all of her latest paperwork mandates, I feel fully justified in doing this."

To Asher's amazement, he promptly sent a punch to his lower rib cage from behind.

Good gravy! Growling in fury, Asher spun around and tackled him.

They crashed to the grass, fists pummeling. The rest of his brothers dog-piled on top of them.

Asher tried to fight them off, but he was outnumbered. It dawned on him in slow degrees that they weren't punching to break ribs, and they were avoiding his face. However, he was getting a brotherly beating that was sure to leave a few bruises.

"Y'all are a bunch of morons." He shoved at every fist and knee he could reach in the effort to drag himself out from beneath their clutches.

"Nope. We're just following the boss's orders," Beldon assured again, waving a short square piece of paper at him. It was the same shade of yellow as the pad of sticky notes he and Bella had traded back and forth while they were dancing.

The first fissure of suspicion worked its way through Asher's chest. "Whose orders?"

"Yours, dude." Beldon slapped the note against the front of his shirt, patted it into place, and stood. "Alright, boys. I think he's had enough."

Amid groans of disappointment, their younger brothers hopped to their feet, yanking shirts into place while dusting the grass and sand off their jeans.

Still glaring at them, Asher ripped the note off his shirt to read it. Sure enough, it was written in the all-too familiar bubbly scrawl of the woman who'd captured his heart.

Someone should slug me for letting Jade come anywhere near me.

They were his words to her from earlier. Snickering despite his soreness, he curled into a sitting position and glanced around the parking lot for her.

She was there in the moonlight, sitting on the open bed of his pickup, smiling sweetly and fluttering her fingers at him.

He grinned despite the bruises rising on nearly every inch of him below his neck. *Game on, woman!* His payback was going to be sweet, so blasted sweet.

She blew a kiss at him and mouthed the words, *I love you.*

Suddenly, all he could think about was the next time those luscious pink lips would be pressed against his.

"Dude, snap out of it!" Cormac snapped his fingers in front of Asher's face as their brothers helped yank him to his feet. One of them had the nerve to try to dust off his backside. He kicked whoever it was out of the way. "It's like she's got you bewitched or something."

Beldon crossed his arms and studied Asher in amusement. "I kind of like this version of him. All dewy eyed and dusty butted." He ducked to avoid the fist Asher swung lazily in his direction. Then he sobered. "Seriously, though, it's good to have you back." His voice grew rough with emotion. "You had us worried for a while there. For way too many weeks and months."

"Yeah. We thought we'd lost you." As Fox joined the conversation, he dashed the back of one scratched and dirty hand across his eyes. It came back muddy with unshed tears.

"Nah, you're never going to lose me." Asher spoke gruffly to hide the emotion festering in his own voice. "I was just a little messed up for a while."

"A little?" Emerson howled, making his twin dissolve into guffaws.

"Yeah, you keep telling yourself that." Beldon leaned in to throw an arm around Asher. "From our angle, you've always been a bit of a jerk."

"What older brother isn't?" Asher retorted mildly.

"You may have a point." Beldon squeezed him hard enough to make him wince, then let go.

"And you always were as ugly as sin," Devlin pointed at the damaged side of Asher's face with a smirk. "Brothers don't give a flying bug's leg about stuff like that."

But they did. Asher met their gazes one by one, overwhelmed by gratitude as he recalled each and every time they'd flown to his defense in the past year. He finally understood that they'd felt his injuries as deeply as he had. His burns, along with the anguish of his recovery, had scored their very souls. Yet his brothers had chosen to walk beside him, every miserable step of the way. It was probably why none of them had dated much lately. They'd been too busy worrying about him. As sure as he was standing in front of them now, he knew he wouldn't have made it this far without their brand of love and loyalty.

"My family," he said quietly. "I don't say it enough, but you guys mean the world to me."

"Blah, blah, sniffle, snort, we get it," Fox drawled in a bored voice, eliciting another round of brotherly snickers.

As they dispersed to their respective vehicles, Asher was left alone with Bella.

"That was some stunt you pulled back there." He pretended to limp his way over to her.

She anxiously scanned his leg. "Are you alright?"

"I will be." Without warning, he leaped up to join her on the open bed of his truck. "You, however, may have a bit of a rocky future ahead."

"Oh?" She giggled as he nipped a trail of kisses along the side of her neck where she was particularly ticklish.

"Yeah. For one thing, paybacks among the Cassidy clan can be a little tough."

"Good thing I'm not a Cassidy," she shot back, smoothing her hands primly down her skirt.

"Yet," he informed her in a husky voice.

Her hands went still in her lap. "Asher?"

"In case you haven't figured it out, darlin', your running days are over." He tucked a handful of hair behind her shoulder. "I have finally met my perfect match, and I'm never going to let you go."

"Asher," she whispered again, this time in wonder.

"I want to sing a few hundred more songs together, watch a few thousand more sunsets with you, and share a few million more kisses."

She blinked back tears, but they looked like happy ones to him. "I can't wait to get started."

"You do realize I'm referring to being your Mr. Right, which will require you to become my Mrs. Right."

"I do."

"Say it again," he commanded softly.

"I do," she said breathlessly.

"And again."

"I do."

He couldn't wait to have her walk down the aisle toward him during that stinking big church wedding his parents were dreaming of (and probably already planning), so the rest of the world could hear her say it, too.

Like this book? Leave a review now!

Ready to find out Jade's next big play for Beldon's heart? She's well aware of the The Unbreakable Rule the Cassidy brothers have against dating each other's leftovers. However, she's always been a firm believer that some rules are made to be broken. Maybe Beldon is right about them being wrong for each other, but they'll never know if she

can't convince him to give whatever is simmering between them a chance in
Mr. Maybe Right for Her.

Much love,
Jo

NOTE FROM JO

Don't worry! There's more to Cassidy Farm, and you don't have to wait until the next book to read it.

Because…*drum roll*…I have some Bonus Content for you. Find out what happened between Jade and

Beldon the day before the fire by signing up for my mailing list. There will be a special bonus content for each COWBOY CONFESSIONS book, just for my subscribers. Also, you'll hear about my next new book as soon as it's out *(plus you get a free book).* Woohoo!

As always, thank you for reading and loving my books!

JOIN CUPPA JO READERS!

If you're on Facebook, please join my group, Cuppa Jo Readers. Don't miss out on the giveaways + all the sweet and swoony cowboys!

https://www.facebook.com/groups/ CuppaJoReaders

GET A FREE BOOK!

Join my mailing list to be the first to know about new releases, free books, special discount prices, and other giveaways.

https://BookHip.com/JNNHTK

SNEAK PREVIEW: MR. MAYBE RIGHT FOR HER

WHEN YOU FALL *in love with the wrong woman and refuse to be the next man she dates and dumps...*

Beldon Cassidy and his brothers have always had each other's backs. Any woman who dates and dumps one of them is off limits to all of them — permanently. Unfortunately, he's been secretly crushing on his oldest brother's ex-girlfriend for years. Though she's single again, she's not available because of The Rule. He's going to have to find a way to turn off his feelings for her before it becomes a problem.

Jade Arletta firmly believes she had no choice but to break up with her boyfriend after unexpectedly losing her heart to one of his brothers. Though she totally respects their loyalty to each other, she doesn't understand why there can't be any exceptions to their silly rule about exes, especially after the brother she ditched soon meets the love of his life. *You're welcome.*

It won't be easy, but she has to find a way to convince this family of cocky cowboys to take her off their black list so she and Beldon can finally snatch a second chance at happily ever after.

A sweet and inspirational, small-town romance with a few Texas-sized detours into comedy!

———

Mr. Maybe Right for Her
Available in eBook, paperback, and Kindle Unlimited!

Mr. Not Right for Her
Mr. Maybe Right for Her
Mr. Right But She Doesn't Know It
Mr. Right Again for Her
Mr. Yeah, Right. As If…

Much love,
Jo

SNEAK PREVIEW: ACCIDENTAL HERO

MATT ROMERO WAS SINGLE AGAIN, and this time he planned to stay that way.

Feeling like the world's biggest fool, he gripped the steering wheel of his white Ford F-150, cruising up the sunny interstate toward Amarillo. He had an interview in the morning, so he was arriving a day early to get the lay of the land. That, and he was anxious to put as many miles as possible between him and his ex.

It was one thing to have allowed himself to become blinded by love. It was another thing entirely to have fallen for the stupidest line in a cheater's handbook.

Cat sitting. I actually allowed her to talk me into cat sitting! Plus, he'd collected his fiancée's mail and carried her latest batch of Amazon deliveries into her condo.

It wasn't that he minded helping out the woman he planned to spend the rest of his life with. What he minded was that she wasn't in New York City on business like she'd claimed. *Nope.* As it turned out, she was nowhere near the Big Apple. It had simply been her cover story for cheating on him, the first lie in a long series of lies.

To make matters worse, she'd recently talked Matt into leaving the Army for her, a decision he'd probably regret for the rest of his life now that she'd broken their engagement and moved on with someone else.

Leaving me single, jobless, and —

The scream of sirens jolted Matt back to the present. A glance in his rearview mirror confirmed his suspicions. He was getting pulled over. *For what?* A scowl down at his speedometer revealed he was cruising at no less than 95 mph. *Whoa!* It was a good twenty miles over the posted speed limit. *Okay, this is bad.* He'd be lucky if he didn't lose his license over this — his fault entirely for driving distracted without his cruise control on. *My day just keeps getting better.*

Slowing and pulling his truck over to the shoulder, he coasted to a stop and waited. And waited. And waited some more. A peek in his side mirror showed the cop was still sitting in his car and talking on his phone.

Oh, come on! Just give me my ticket already.

To stop the pounding between his temples, Matt reached for the red cooler he'd propped on the passenger seat and pulled out a can of soda. He popped the tab and tipped it up to chug down a shot of caffeine. He hadn't slept much the last couple of nights.

Before he could take a second sip, movement in the rearview mirror caught his attention. He watched as the police officer finally opened his door, unfolded his large frame from the front seat of his black SUV, and stood. However, he continued talking on his phone instead of walking Matt's way.

Are you kidding me? Matt swallowed a dry chuckle and took another swig of his soda. It was a good thing he'd hit the road the day before his interview at the Pantex nuclear plant. At the rate his day was going, it might take the rest of the afternoon to collect his speeding ticket.

He'd reached the outskirts of Amarillo, only about twenty to thirty miles from his final destination. The exit sign for Hereford was up ahead. Or the Beef Capital of the World, as the small farm town was often called.

He reached across the dashboard to open his glove compartment and fish out his registration card and proof of insurance. His gut told him there wasn't going to be any talking his way out of this one. As a general rule, men in blue didn't sympathize with folks going twenty miles or more over the speed limit.

Digging for his wallet, he pulled out his driver's license. Out of sheer habit, he reached inside the slot where he normally kept his military ID and found it empty. *Right.* He no longer possessed one, which left him with an oddly empty feeling.

He took another gulp of soda and watched as the officer pocketed his cell phone. *Finally! Guess that means it's time to get this party started.* Matt chunked his soda can into the nearest cup holder and stuck his driver's license, truck registration, and insurance card between two fingers. Hitting an automatic button on the door, he lowered his window a few inches and waited.

The guy strode up to Matt's truck window with a bit of a swagger. His tan Stetson was pulled low over his eyes. "License and registration, soldier."

Guess you noticed the Ranger tab on my license plate. Matt wordlessly poked the requested items through the window opening.

"Any reason you're in such a hurry this morning?" the officer mused curiously as he scanned Matt's identification. He was so tall, he had to stoop to peer through the window. Like Matt, he had a dark tan, brown hair, and a goatee. The two of them could've passed as cousins or something.

"Nothing worth hearing, officer." *My problem. Not yours. Don't want to talk about it.* Matt squinted through the glaring sun to read the guy's name on his tag. *McCarty.*

"That's too bad, because I always have plenty of time to chat when I'm writing up such a hefty ticket." Officer McCarty's tone was mildly sympathetic, though it was impossible to read his expression behind his sunglasses. "I clocked you going twenty-two miles over the posted limit, Mr. Romero."

Twenty-two miles? Yeah, that's not good. Not good at

all. Matt's jaw tightened, and he could feel the veins in his temples throbbing. It looked like he was going to have to share his story, after all. Maybe, just maybe, the trooper would feel so sorry for him that he'd give him a warning instead of a ticket. It was worth a try, anyway. *If nothing else, it'll give you something to laugh about during your next coffee break.*

"Today was supposed to be my wedding day." He spoke through stiff lips, finding a strange sort of relief in confessing that sorry fact to a perfect stranger. Fortunately, they'd never have to see each other again.

"I'm sorry for your loss." Officer McCarty glanced up from Matt's license to give him what felt like a piercing once over. He was probably trying to gauge if he was telling the truth or not.

"Oh, she's still alive," Matt muttered. "Found somebody else, that's all." He gripped the steering wheel and drummed his thumbs against it. *I'm just the poor fool she cheated on.*

He was so done with dating. At the moment, he couldn't imagine ever again putting his heart on the chopping block of love. *Better to be lonely than to let another person destroy you like that.* She'd taken everything from him that mattered — his pride, his dignity, even his career.

"Ouch," Officer McCarty sighed. "Well, here comes the tough part about my job. Despite your reasons for speeding, you were putting lives at risk. Your own included."

"Can't disagree with that." Matt stared straight

ahead, past the small spidery nick in his windshield. He'd gotten hit by a rock earlier while passing a semi tractor trailer. It really hadn't been his day. Or his week. Or his year, for that matter. It didn't mean he was going to grovel, though. He'd tried to appeal to the guy's sympathy and failed. The sooner he gave him his ticket, the sooner they could both be on their way.

A massive dump truck on the oncoming side of the highway abruptly swerved into the narrow, grassy median. It was a few hundred yards away, but the front left tire dipped down, *way* down, making the truck pitch heavily to one side.

"Whoa!" Matt shouted, pointing to get Officer McCarty's attention. "That guy looks like he's in trouble!"

Two vehicles on Matt's side of the road passed him in quick succession — a rusty blue van pulling a fifth wheel and a shiny red Dodge Ram.

When Officer McCarty didn't respond, Matt laid on his horn to warn the two drivers, just as the dump truck started to roll. It was like watching a horror movie in slow motion, knowing something bad was about to happen while being helpless to stop it.

The dump truck slammed onto its side and skidded noisily across Matt's lane. The blue van whipped to the right shoulder in a vain attempt to avoid the collision. Matt winced as the van's bumper caught the hood of the skidding dump truck nearly head on, then jack-knifed into the air.

The driver of the red truck was only a few car

lengths behind, jamming so hard on its brakes that it left two dark smoking lines of rubber on the pavement. Seconds later, it careened into the median and flipped on its side. It wasn't immediately clear if the red pickup had collided with any part of the dump truck. However, an ominous swirl of smoke seeped from beneath its hood.

For a split second, Matt and Officer McCarty stared in shock at each other. Then the officer shoved Matt's license and registration back through the opening in the window. "Looks like I've got more important things to do than give you a ticket." He sprinted toward his SUV, leaped inside, and gunned it toward the scene of the accident with his lights flashing and sirens blaring. He only drove a short distance before stopping his vehicle and canting it across both lanes to form a makeshift blockade.

Though Matt was no longer in the military, his defend-and-protect instincts kicked in. There was no telling how long it would take the emergency vehicles to arrive, and he didn't like the way the red pickup was smoking. The driver hadn't climbed out of the cab yet, either, which wasn't a good sign.

Officer McCarty reached the blue van first, probably because it was the closest, and assisted a dazed man from one of the back passenger seats. He led him to the side of the road, helped him get seated on a small incline, then jogged back to help the driver exit the van. Unfortunately, the officer was only one man, and this was much bigger than a one-man job.

Following his gut instincts, Matt disengaged his

emergency brake and gunned his way up the shoulder, pausing beside the officer's vehicle. Turning off his motor, he leaped from his truck and jogged across the highway to the red pickup. The motor was still running, and the smoke was rising more thickly now.

Whoever was behind the wheel needed to get out immediately before the thing caught fire or exploded. Matt took a flying leap to hop on top of the cab and crawl to the driver's door. It was locked.

Pounding on the window, he shouted at the driver, "You okay in there?"

There was no answer and no movement. Peering closer, he could make out the unmoving figure of a woman. Blonde, pale, and curled to one side. The only thing holding her in place was the strap of a seatbelt around her waist. A trickle of red ran across one cheek.

Matt's survival training kicked in. Crouching over the side of the truck, he quickly assessed the undamaged windshield and decided it wasn't the best entry point. *Too bad.* Because his only other option was to shower the driver with glass. *Sorry, lady!* Swinging a leg, he jabbed the heel of his boot into the section of window nearest the lock. By some miracle, he managed to pop a fist-sized hole instead of shattering the entire pane.

Reaching inside, he unlocked the door and pulled it open. The next part was a little trickier, since he had to reach down, *way* down, to unbuckle the woman and catch her weight before she fell. It would've been easier if she were conscious and able to follow his instructions.

Guess I'll have to do it without any help. An ominous hiss of steam and smoke from beneath the hood stiffened his resolve and made him move faster.

"Come on, lady," he muttered, releasing her seatbelt and catching her slender frame before she fell. With a grunt of exertion, he hefted her free of the mangled cab. Then he half-slid, half hopped back to the ground with her in his arms. As soon as his boots hit the pavement, he took off at a jog.

She was lighter than he'd been expecting. Her upper arm, that his left hand was cupped around, felt desperately thin despite her baggy pink and plaid shirt. One long, strawberry blonde braid dangled over her shoulder, and a sprinkle of freckles stood out in stark relief against her pale cheeks.

She didn't so much as twitch as he ran with her, telling him that she was still out cold. He hoped it didn't mean she'd hit her head too hard on impact. Visions of traumatic brain injuries and their long list of complications swarmed through his mind, along with the possibility that he might've just finished moving a woman with a broken neck or back. *Please don't let that be the case, Lord.*

He carried her to the far right shoulder and up a grassy knoll where Officer McCarty was depositing the other injured victims. A dry wind gusted, sending a layer of fine dust in their direction. One prickly, rolling tumbleweed followed. On the other side of the knoll was a rocky canyon wall that went straight up, underscoring the fact that there really hadn't been any way for the hapless van and pickup drivers to avoid the collision. They'd literally been trapped between the canyon and oncoming traffic.

An explosion ricocheted through the air, shaking the ground beneath Matt's feet. On pure instinct, he dove for the grass, using his body to shield the woman in his arms. He used one hand to cradle her head against his chest and his other hand to break their fall as best he could.

A few of the other injured drivers and passengers cried out in fear as smoke billowed around them and blanketed the scene. For the next few minutes, it was difficult to see much, though the wave of ensuing heat had a suffocating feel to it. The woman beneath Matt remained motionless, though he thought he heard her mumble something at one point. He continued to crouch over her, keeping her head cradled beneath his hand. He rubbed his thumb beneath her nose and determined she was still breathing. However, she remained unconscious. He debated what to do next.

A fire engine howled in the distance, making his shoulders slump in relief. Help had finally arrived. More sirens blared, and the area was soon crawling with fire engines, ambulances, and paramedics with stretchers. One walked determinedly in his direction.

"Hi! My name is Star, and I'm here to help you. What's your name, sir?" the EMT worker inquired in a calm, even tone. Her chin-length dark hair was blowing nearly sideways in the wind. She shook her head to knock it away, revealing a pair of snapping dark eyes swimming with concern.

"I'm Sergeant Matt Romero," he informed her out of sheer habit. *Well, maybe no longer the sergeant part.* "Don't worry about me. I'm fine. This woman is not. I don't know her name. She was unconscious when I pulled her out of her truck."

As the curvy EMT stepped closer, Matt could read her name tag. *Corrigan.* "Like I said, I'm here to do everything I can to help." Her forehead wrinkled in alarm as she caught sight of the injured woman's face. "Omigosh! Bree?" Tossing her red medical bag on the ground, she slid to her knees beside the two of them. "Oh, Bree, honey!" she sighed, reaching for her pulse.

"I-I..." The woman stirred. Her lashes fluttered a few times against her cheeks. Then they snapped open, revealing two pools of the deepest blue Matt had ever seen. Though glazed with pain, her gaze latched anxiously onto him. "Don't leave me," she pleaded with a hitch in her voice.

There was something oddly personal about the request. Though he was sure they'd never met before, she spoke as if she recognized him. Her confusion tugged at every one of his heartstrings, making him long to grant her request.

"I won't," he promised huskily, hardly knowing what he was saying. In that moment, he probably would have said anything to make the desperate look in her eyes go away.

"I'm not liking her heart rate." Star produced a

penlight and flipped it on. Shining it in one of her friend's eyes, then the other, she cried urgently, "Bree? It's me, Star. Can you tell me what happened, hon?"

A shiver worked its way through Bree's too-thin frame. "Don't leave me," she whispered again to Matt, before her eyelids fluttered closed. Another shiver worked its way through her, despite the fact that she was no longer conscious.

"She's going into shock." Star glanced worriedly over her shoulder. "Need a stretcher over here," she called sharply. One was swiftly rolled their way.

Matt helped the EMT lift and deposit their precious burden on it.

"Can you make it to the hospital?" Star asked as he helped push the stretcher toward the nearest ambulance. "Bree seemed pretty insistent about you sticking around."

Matt's eyebrows shot upward in surprise. He hadn't been expecting yet another person he'd never met before to ask him to stick around. "Uh, sure." In her delirium, the injured woman had probably mistaken him for someone else. However, he didn't mind helping out. *Who knows?* Maybe he could give the attending physician some information about her rescue that might prove useful in her treatment.

Or maybe he was just drawn to the fragile-looking Bree for reasons he couldn't explain. What-ever the case, Matt suddenly wasn't feeling in a terrible hurry to hit the road again. Fortunately, he had plenty of extra time built into his schedule before his interview tomorrow. The only real task he had left for the day was finding a hotel room once he reached Amarillo.

"I just need to let Officer McCarty know I'm leaving the scene of the accident." Matt shook his head sheepishly. "I kinda hate to admit this, but he had me pulled over for speeding before everything went down here." He waved a hand at the carnage around them. It was a dismal scene, punctuated by twisted metal and scorched pavement. All three mangled vehicles looked like they were totaled.

Star snickered, then seemed to catch herself. "Sorry. That was inappropriate laughter. Very inappropriate laughter."

He shrugged, not the least bit offended. A lot of people laughed when they were nervous or upset, which Star clearly had been since the moment she'd discovered the unconscious woman was a friend. "It was pretty stupid of me to be driving these long, empty stretches of highway without my cruise control on." Especially with the way he'd been brooding non-stop for the past seventy-two hours.

Star shot him a sympathetic look. "Believe me, I'm not judging. Far from it." She reached out to pat Officer McCarty's arm as they passed by him with the stretcher. "The only reason a bunch of us in Hereford don't have a lot more points on our licenses is because we grew up with this sweet guy."

"Oh, no! Is that Bree?" Officer McCarty groaned. He pulled his sunglasses down to take a closer look over the top of his lenses. His stoic expression was gone. In its place was one etched with worry. The personal kind. Like Star, he knew the victim.

"Yeah." Star's pink glossy lips twisted. "She and her brother can't catch a break, can they?"

Since two more paramedics converged on them to help lift Bree's stretcher into the ambulance, Matt paused to face the trooper who'd pulled him over.

"Any issues with me following them to the hospital, officer? Star asked me if I would." Unfortunately, it would give the guy more time and opportunity to ticket Matt, but that couldn't be helped.

"Emmitt," Officer McCarty corrected. "The name is Emmitt, alright? I think you more than worked off your ticket back there."

Sucking in a breath of relief, Matt held out a hand. "Thanks, man. I really appreciate it." It was a huge concession. The guy could've taken his license if he'd wanted to.

They soberly shook hands, eyeing each other.

"You need me to come by the PD to file a witness report or anything before I boogie out of town this evening?" Matt pressed.

"Nah. Just give me a call, and we'll take care of it over the phone." Emmitt produced a business card and handed it over. "Not sure if we'll need your story, since I saw it go down, but we should probably still cross every T."

"Roger that." Matt stuffed the card in the back pocket of his jeans.

"Where are you headed, anyway?"

"Amarillo. Got an interview at Pantex tomorrow."

"Nice! It's a solid company." Emmitt nodded. "I've got several friends who work there."

Star leaned out from the back of the ambulance. "You coming or what?" she called impatiently to Matt.

He nodded vigorously. "I'll follow you," he called back and jogged back to his truck. Since the ambulance was on the opposite side of the highway, he turned on his blinker and put his oversized tires to good use while traversing the median. He had to spin his wheels a bit in the center of the median to get his tires to grab the sandy incline leading to the other side. He was grateful all over again that he'd splurged on a few upgrades for his truck to make it fit for off-roading.

He followed the ambulance north and found himself driving the final twenty minutes or so to Amarillo, probably because it boasted a much bigger hospital than any of the smaller surrounding towns — more than one, actually. Due to another vehicle leaving the parking lot as he was entering it, Matt was able to grab a decently close parking spot. He jogged into the waiting room, dropped Star Corrigan's name a few times, and tried to make it sound like he was a close friend of the patient.

Looking doubtful, the receptionist made him wait while she paged Star, who appeared a short time later to escort him into the emergency room. "Bree's in Bay 6," she informed him in a strained voice, reaching for his arm and practically dragging him behind the curtain.

If anything, Bree looked even thinner and more fragile than she had outside on the highway. A nurse was stooped over her, inserting an I.V. into her arm.

"She still hasn't woken up." Star's voice was soft, barely above a whisper. "They're pretty sure she has a concussion. Sounds like they're gonna run a full battery of tests to figure out what's going on."

Matt nodded, not knowing what to say.

The lovely EMT's pager went off. She snatched it up and scowled at it. "I just got another call. It's a busy day out there for motorists." She texted a message on her cell phone, then cast him a sideways glance. "Any chance you'll be able to stick around until Bree's brother gets here?"

That's when it hit Matt that this had been the EMT's real goal all along — to ensure that her friend wasn't left alone. She'd known she could get called away to the next job at any second.

"Not a problem." He offered what he hoped was a reassuring smile. Amarillo was where he'd been heading, so he'd already reached his final destination. "I wasn't planning on going far, anyway. Got an interview at Pantex in the morning."

"No kidding! Well, good luck with that," she returned with a curious, searching look. "A lot of my friends moved up this way for jobs after high school."

Officer Emmitt McCarty had said something similar. "Hey, ah…" Matt hated detaining the EMT any longer than necessary, but it might not hurt to know a few more details about the unconscious woman, since he was about to be alone with her. "Mind telling me Bree's last name?"

"Anderson. Her brother is Brody. Brody Anderson. They run a ranch about halfway between here and Hereford, so it'll take him a good twenty to thirty minutes to get here."

"It's alright. I can stay. It was nice meeting you, by the way." His gaze landed on Bree's left hand, which was resting limply atop the white blankets on her bed. She wasn't wearing a wedding ring. *Not that it matters. I'm a complete idiot for looking.* He forced his gaze back to the EMT. "Sorry about the circumstances, of course."

"Me, too." She shot another worried look at her friend and dropped her voice conspiratorially. "Hey, you're really not supposed to be back here since you're not family, but I sorta begged and they sorta agreed to overlook the rules until Brody gets here." She eyed him worriedly.

"Don't worry." He could tell she hated the necessity of leaving. "I'll stick around until her brother gets here, even if I get booted out to the waiting room with the regular Joes."

"Thanks! Really." She whipped out her cell phone. "Here's my number in case you need to reach me for anything."

Wow! Matt had not been expecting the beautiful EMT to offer him her phone number. Not that he was complaining. It was a boost to his sorely damaged ego. He dug for his phone. "I'm ready when you're ready."

She rattled off her number, and he quickly texted her back so she would have his.

"Take care of her for me, will you, Matt?" she pleaded anxiously.

On second thought, there was nothing flirtatious about Star's demeanor. It was entirely possible that their exchange of phone numbers was exactly what she'd claimed it was — a means of staying in touch about the status of her friend's condition. Giving her a reassuring look, Matt fist-bumped her.

Looking grateful, she pushed aside the curtain and was gone. The nurse followed, presumably to report Bree's vitals to the doctor on duty.

Matt moved to the foot of the hospital bed. "So, who do you think I am, Bree?" *And why did you beg me not to leave you?*

Her long blonde lashes remained motionless against her cheeks. It looked like he was going to have to stick around for a while if he wanted answers.

———

Hope you enjoyed this excerpt from
Accidental Hero.
Available in eBook, paperback, hard cover large print, and Kindle Unlimited!

The whole alphabet is coming — read them all!
A - Accidental Hero
B - Best Friend Hero

C - Celebrity Hero

D - Damaged Hero

E - Enemies to Hero

F - Forbidden Hero

G - Guardian Hero

H - Hunk and Hero

I - Instantly Her Hero

J - Jilted Hero

K - Kissable Hero

L - Long Distance Hero

M - Mistaken Hero

N - Not Good Enough Hero

Much love,

Jo

SNEAK PREVIEW: WINDS OF CHANGE

GETTING HIRED *as a high school principal in her hometown is her biggest dream come true, except for one small detail — her ex runs the security team.*

During her teen years, Hope Remington was the darling of Heart Lake, and Josh Hawling was...well, bad news on the rough side of town. And now she's returning as head principal to unite their two rival high schools under one roof. She soon realizes that her biggest challenge isn't the gangs embedded in the student body. It's Josh, who's somehow convinced their aging superintendent that he and his security firm partner can keep the campus safe while coaching a bunch of farm boys into a football team that'll make the playoffs.

Hope wonders how she's supposed to improve test scores and graduation rates when her students' biggest idol is a man who spent more time in the principal's office than in the classroom. Even though she feels safer having Josh on their crime-ridden campus, she's not looking forward to her daily encounters with the cocky head of security. Or being socked in the heart all over again by his devastating smile. Or having to finally face her unwanted attraction to him that might have kindled into a lot more if she'd never left Texas in the first place.

Welcome to Heart Lake! A small town teaming with old family rivalries and the rumble of horses' hooves — faith-filled romance that you'll never forget.

———

Heart Lake #1: Winds of Change
Available in eBook, paperback, and Kindle Unlimited!

Read them all!
Winds of Change
Song of Nightingales
Perils of Starlight
Return of Miracles
Thousands of Gifts
Race of Champions
Storm of Secrets
Season of Angels
Clash of Hearts
Mountain of Fire

Much love,
Jo

SNEAK PREVIEW: HER BILLIONAIRE BOSS

WHEN THE CEO *of a mega corporation hires the daughter of his family's biggest rival to serve as his personal assistant...*

Jacey Maddox decides to do her part to end her family's decades-old feud with Genesis & Sons by going to work for them. That is, if they'll consider hiring a hated Maddox...

CEO Luca Calcagni is determined to teach the rebel youngest daughter of his family's oldest rival the lesson of her life by agreeing to her foolish request for a job. He gives her a punishing schedule with one goal in mind — to send her running. However, he gets schooled in return when she bravely holds her ground, rekindling his secret attraction to her that he'd mistakenly assumed he was over.

A man known as a cobra in the boardroom isn't supposed to fall for the enemy, and two very powerful families are guaranteed to disapprove if he pursues a second chance at love.

———

Her Billionaire Boss
Available in eBook, paperback, and Kindle Unlimited!

BLACK TIE BILLIONAIRES SERIES
Complete series — read them all!
Her Billionaire Boss
Her Billionaire Bodyguard
Her Billionaire Secret Admirer
Her Billionaire Best Friend
Her Billionaire Geek
Her Billionaire Double Date
Black Tie Billionaires Box Set #1 (Books 1-3)
Black Tie Billionaires Box Set #2 (Books 4-6)

Much love,
Jo

ALSO BY JO GRAFFORD

For the most up-to-date printable list of my books:

Click here

or go to:

https://www.JoGrafford.com/books

For the most up-to-date printable list of books by Jo Grafford, writing as Jovie Grace *(sweet historical romance)*:

Click here

or go to:

https://www.jografford.com/joviegracebooks

ABOUT JO

Jo is an Amazon bestselling author of sweet and inspirational romance stories about faith, hope, love and family drama with a few Texas-sized detours into comedy.

1.) Follow on Amazon!
amazon.com/author/jografford

2.) Join Cuppa Jo Readers!
https://www.facebook.com/groups/
CuppaJoReaders

3.) Follow on Bookbub!
https://www.bookbub.com/authors/jo-grafford

4.) Follow on YouTube
https://www.youtube.com/channel/
UC3R1at97Qso6BXiBIxCjQ5w